I0517139

MILES LEDOUX

VIOLET

Winter in Veil, Book 1

First published by ABCs 2025

Copyright © 2025 by Miles Ledoux

All rights reserved. No part of this publication may be reproduced, stored or transmitted in any form or by any means, electronic, mechanical, photocopying, recording, scanning, or otherwise without written permission from the publisher. It is illegal to copy this book, post it to a website, or distribute it by any other means without permission.

This novel is entirely a work of fiction. The names, characters and incidents portrayed in it are the work of the author's imagination. Any resemblance to actual persons, living or dead, events or localities is entirely coincidental.

First edition

ISBN: 978-1-882508-81-5

Cover art by Rachel Kelli
Editing by Julie Mianecki

This book was professionally typeset on Reedsy.
Find out more at reedsy.com

Preface

All around the cobbler's bench
The monkey chased the weasel
The monkey thought 'twas all in fun
Pop! goes the weasel

Prologue

None of the children in Veil had ever seen a dead body.

It was an October Friday, just after school let out for the day. Normally school lasted till mid-afternoon, but today was a half-day; the students hadn't even had lunch yet. Most of them headed for the school buses lined up in a slanted row beside the courtyard, while a few dozen began to gather in small clusters along the side of the building.

One nine-year-old girl with blond hair broke from her cluster as a boy her age approached. "Neil, come on! We're waiting for you! We're gonna get ice cream!"

Their group complete, the children trooped across the courtyard. Some of them zipped up their long-sleeved jackets. The farther they got from the rumbling school bus engines, the more palpably they could feel Vermont's fifty-degree weather.

On most school days, parents imposed a strict rule that their children must be home by a certain hour in the afternoon, so a half-day gave the kids some time to stop for a treat. Sadly, however, as the group approached the ice cream shop…

"Aw, man!" Emma exclaimed in dismay. "It's closed!"

"They must've just closed for the season," lamented Kirsten, who was a head taller than the rest and prone to pretending she was older, too.

In low spirits, they crossed Main Street, left behind the old, narrow, brick buildings that housed most of Veil's local businesses, and shuffled along through neighborhoods of Victorian-style houses of varying colors.

"Wow," Neil remarked as they passed a red two-story house where, in the space of the morning, twenty pumpkins had materialized all over, even on the roof.

"I heard the deputy mayor has a giant pumpkin growing on her front lawn," said a boy named Chris. Neil tilted his head back and squinted at the foothills up ahead, which formed the edge of town. Chris barked out a laugh. "You can't see it from here! It's not *that* big." Neil turned red and looked down.

"We can see the lights of Mr. Pressler's mansion from our house," said Emma.

"My dad says the people who live on the sides of the mountain like to turn on their lights at night to remind us that they have more money than we do," said Kirsten.

The children's pace slowed as the sidewalk climbed a gentle incline toward the houses nestled at the base of the foothills. A silence fell over them, perhaps born of despondency over their missed treat.

All of a sudden, at a bend in the road, one of them pointed and exclaimed, "Snowflake!"

It was true. High up in the air, bright white against the dark green of the trees on the mountainside, a big, fluffy snowflake was drifting down, fluttering this way and that. As one, the children shot from the sidewalk and onto the grass, where the tree line neared the pavement. The first snowflake of winter was something of a big deal in Veil. If one of them could catch the snowflake on their tongue…

It was a mad scramble there at the edge of the woods, with everyone shoving each other, necks craned upward, eyes strained, tongues out, stretching as high as they could. If the snowflake sensed its doom, it didn't seem too bothered by it. It tumbled lazily down, rolling over, to and fro, on the air currents. A gloved hand reached up—

"You can't use hands!! It has to land right on your tongue for it to count!"

Kirsten almost won the prize, but she exhaled at the wrong moment, sending the snowflake zooming toward her shorter comrades. Neil cried out and covered his face.

"Did it get in your eye?"

"It went up my *nose!!*" The lot of them burst into laughter. "Does it still count?" Neil wanted to know.

The excitement over, in high spirits they proceeded along the sidewalk, away from the trees. It was a good thing the snowflake had not blown into the forest; if it had, the kids would have been breaking a rule by going in after it. None of them was allowed to play in the woods unsupervised.

Neil said that the inside of his nose had never felt so cold before. He was worried about getting brain freeze.

Then Kirsten stopped and said, "Hey…where's Emma?"

One by one, they turned on the spot. They spread out a little, staring down the road, past houses, around trees.

"Emma?"

"Emma?!"

"Is she hiding?"

"There's nowhere to hide."

"Where did she go??"

"Did she just leave us?"

"Without us seeing? I don't think so."

"She always says goodbye to us."

"Was she still with us when we ran after the snowflake?" An abrupt, grim silence met Neil's question. Each child played back

3

the memory of Emma pointing and shouting, "Snowflake!" All of them had instantly rushed toward it, their eyes on the prize, blind to everything else. Anything could have happened to Emma and they wouldn't have seen.

Quickly they backtracked the way they'd come, down the sidewalk to the bend in the road that nearly bordered the edge of the woods. They peered in, squinting.

"Emma?" one of them called. There was no answer.

"Emma!" another of them tried, more loudly. The only response was the wind whistling as it picked up speed.

Neil asked, "Should we go in and look for her?"

The kids looked at each other and didn't answer.

Here at the edge of the forest, the trees were spaced far apart, but the further you went in, it was all bushes and trunks and pine needles pressed against each other. None of them would be able to go in that far and still be able to see all around.

Swallowing, Kirsten said, "No, we should get a grown-up. Who lives closest?" One of the other girls timidly raised her hand. Kirsten pointed at her. "You guys go with her and tell her parents. I'll stay here in case Emma...comes back or...calls for help."

"I'll stay, too," said Neil.

Suddenly Chris pointed: "Wait, there she is!"

He must have had good eyesight, for the others couldn't see anything. He was pointing into the woods. They squinted and craned their necks. "Where?"

"Right there!"

Finally, the others spotted her. She was coming out of the woods toward them. At first they had only glimpses of her as she wove between the trees, passing in and out of their field of view—her blond hair, her silver jacket, her fuchsia backpack.

Finally, she emerged from the woods where they could see her fully.

"Emma," said Kirsten, "are you okay?"

She did not look okay. She wouldn't look any of them in the eye. Her eyes stared straight ahead and down, almost expressionless. Her mouth was parted and she was breathing heavily, though not from exertion. Concerned, one of her friends reached out to touch her and she flinched, trembling.

"Emma…?"

Emma ran. With all of her friends staring after her she ran, full tilt, into the street and up the road and out of sight.

She didn't stop running till she reached her house. She ran in through the garage and into the kitchen by the side door. Her mother was inside, making a red velvet cake in the shape of a human heart, as practice for the upcoming Halloween baking contest. "Hi, honey," she cooed. "How was school?"

For a moment Emma stood where she was, still staring ahead, wide-eyed, at something that wasn't there. Her mother had her back to her, mixing ingredients in a bowl. When Emma didn't answer, she glanced over at her. Seeing her mother's face made Emma blink, and perhaps out of habit, she answered, "It was good."

"Good!" Her mother turned back to her mixing bowl. "Did they give you any homework for the weekend?"

Emma took a deep breath. "I…"

"What was that?"

Emma gulped. "I found a dead body."

Emma's mother decided she needed to add more red food coloring, but the bottle on the counter was empty. She began searching the cabinets. "Found a what?"

"A dead body. A girl."

"Oh, were you guys playing *CSI* again?"

Emma shook her head dully.

"Aha!" Her mother found some behind the oregano.

"I think she was a little older than me."

"Than *I*," her mother automatically corrected her.

"A little older than I."

"There you go." Shaking the bottle over the bowl, she bestowed a generous amount of red food coloring on the mixture. "Yes!" she said to herself. "Much more like blood."

Emma turned a little green at the word. Mechanically she took off her shoes and went out, heading for her bedroom.

A minute later, Emma's father came in. "Was that Emma? Is she home?"

"Yep," said her mother.

"Oh, good." He let out a breath of relief.

His wife turned to him, still mixing. "What's the matter?"

He showed her his phone. "There's an amber alert. Just got a text. Little girl missing. The sheriff and his deputies are all out looking for her. Just wanted to make sure ours was home safe—are you all right?"

His wife had gone completely still, her eyes like saucers, one hand on the edge of the bowl, the other on the big spoon, mid-stir. She stayed that way for a few seconds, then, like a bullet from a gun, she abandoned the cake mixture and barreled past her husband, calling, "Emma! *Emma!!*"

I

H elp...
    Help me...
    I hurt... Everything hurts...
  What happened to me? Can't remember...

Blurry. Too blurry to see. Something in my eyes.

Hair. Hair in my eyes. Need to move it.

Moving...hurts...

There. Can see trees. Trees means...outside. On the ground. Lying on the ground.

Noise. Sticks cracking. Dirt crunching.

Someone walking. Coming toward me. Getting closer.

Help me.

Can't speak. Hurts too much.

A shadow. Someone standing over me. Looking at me. Staring.

Help. Please help.

No, don't. Don't go. Please don't go. Where are you going? Come back...

Have to go after her. Need to go after her.

Moving hurts...hurts so much...

If you don't go after her, you'll die.

Oh God.

YEEEAAARRRGH—

* * *

"You okay?"

Deputy Jen Grogan glanced over at Sheriff Keith Dubowski and realized they were parked in front of the Thurmins' house. She'd been so lost in her own thoughts, she hadn't noticed when they arrived. She sighed gloomily. "No," she replied. "I don't know how I'm ever going to tell my daughter about this."

"She and Megan were friends?"

Grogan closed her eyes for a moment. "Megan's practically the only friend Cyanne has made since we moved here."

The sheriff looked surprised. "I thought she signed up for Outward Bound last month. Didn't she make any friends there?"

Grogan shook her head. "She'd barely started before she quit. Same as the thing before that. She avoids anything that would bring her into contact with more people. I'm worried about her."

Mr. Thurmin appeared on the front porch, guiding a little blond girl by the hand. Her eyes were blotchy; she'd probably been crying.

"Maybe the body in the woods isn't Megan's," Grogan suddenly said, hopefully. "I mean, Megan was last seen in Wenskee Woods, and that's on the opposite side of town, so maybe—"

"Maybe we have a dead girl *and* another one who's missing?" The sheriff gave her a look that was sympathetic but stern. Grogan winced, inwardly chastising herself. She tried to pull herself out of her dread, to focus on the task at hand rather than on having to tell Cy that her friend was gone. *Like I had to tell Cy about her father...*

"Come on," the sheriff said gently.

As they alighted from the patrol car, a second one pulled up

8

behind them and Deputy James Derrick appeared. He got out and put on his wide-brimmed deputy's hat. Then, when he saw that the sheriff wasn't wearing a hat, he quickly tossed it back into the car.

The three of them approached the porch. The sheriff nodded to the father. "Frank," he greeted him. Frank Thurmin led the little girl down the steps. Dubowski, tall, bearded, and barrel-chested, squatted so that he was at eye-level with the girl. "Hello, Emma," he said mildly. "My name is Sheriff Dubowski. You can call me Keith if you want."

Emma cleared her throat. "Hi," she said, and waved.

Casually the sheriff went on, "Your parents just called me and said you'd found something in the woods."

"I found a dead body," Emma said promptly, without inflection. Grogan and Derrick exchanged glances.

"Uh-huh. And it was a little girl? Like you?"

"She was a little bigger than me. Than I," Emma corrected herself. Then it appeared that the trauma was starting to wear off, for she said, "I can show her to you if you want."

Her father gave the sheriff a quick look, the meaning of which was plain: *No way.*

"That's okay, you don't have to see her again," the sheriff replied, "but it would help if you could point us in the—"

"Come on." Emma grabbed the sheriff's hand and started leading him down the sidewalk. Frank stammered out half a protest before he gave up and followed them.

Grogan couldn't help but smirk. Both of her own daughters had been precocious at that age. She threw an amused glance at James Derrick, but rather than return it, Derrick shot her a glower of disapproval before he turned away, following the others. Trailing behind, Grogan restrained a sigh.

Despite her best efforts since she'd moved here, she was still on Derrick's bad side. Part of her couldn't blame him; after all, he'd been in line to succeed sixty-something-year-old Hal as senior deputy once Hal retired, or so everyone had assumed. Then Grogan had contacted the sheriff and told him she was moving back to Veil with her teenage daughter, and asked if he had any open positions in his department. Jen Grogan and Keith Dubowski had worked together years ago, had even more or less grown up together (though he was thirteen years her senior). Knowing she had, elsewhere, proven herself a more than capable law officer, Dubowski offered Grogan the imminently vacant position of senior deputy, and she'd accepted. Thus Derrick found himself passed over for someone who was, to him, a complete stranger. No wonder he resented her. Still, it had been four months; he had to get over it sooner or later.

Emma led them down the street to the bend in the road, where she let go of the sheriff's hand and pointed through the trees. "She's behind the big log."

The sheriff glanced at his deputies and they followed him into the forest. They had to be careful where they stepped, the ground was so cluttered with rocks, roots, bushes, and dead branches. Grogan wondered what had possessed Emma to come into the forest far enough to find the body. Being smaller, it might have been easier for the girl to squeeze past all the obstacles, but surely not by much.

The difficult passage made the distance seem longer, but it was actually only a few meters until they found the log Emma had mentioned. They paused. The sheriff glanced again at his deputies, giving them a silent warning to prepare themselves. Grogan had seen corpses before, but never a dead child. She'd told her daughters time and again that the monsters in nightmares weren't real, and Megan's mother had probably told her the same thing. She tried not to think about how horrible it had been for Megan in her final moments.

Shoving all her emotions away—apart from determination to do her job—she stepped around the log along with her colleagues.

They stared, looked at each other, then stared down again.

There was nothing there. No body, nothing.

"Maybe she forgot where she found it," suggested Derrick, starting off in another direction.

The sheriff's hand lashed out and seized Derrick before he could take another step, then gently pulled him back. The sheriff squatted and peered at a young pine. He leaned his head from side to side, then nodded. "Yup. Blood." He pointed to a low branch. "See?"

Grogan squinted and absolutely could not make out anything whatsoever, but she trusted Dubowski's keen senses. He had been a forest ranger before he became a sheriff. She was also sure Derrick couldn't see anything, even as the younger deputy said fervently, "Yeah, I see it."

"Was she dragged off?" Grogan asked.

The sheriff shook his head and pointed at a mass of broken twigs nearby. "She crawled this way, then she stood up and kept going." He rose and peered past the twigs. "Beyond that, I'm not a good enough tracker to tell what she did. But she's alive, all right."

Grogan breathed a quick sigh of relief.

The sheriff shot her a serious look. "For now."

He led them back out of the forest. He went straight to Emma and knelt in front of her. "Emma," he said, "the girl you found isn't there anymore. We think she's still alive. I need you to tell me, how hurt did she look? Was she bleeding?"

With a look of bewilderment, Emma nodded.

"Where was she bleeding? On her chest? Her head?"

"Her head." Emma touched the side of her forehead. "And on her fingers."

The sheriff squeezed Emma's shoulder, muttered a quick "Thank you" to her father, and went off to speak urgently into his radio.

As Dubowski ordered a new search pattern, Grogan approached Emma and bent over to speak to her. "Emma, what made you go into the forest in the first place?"

Emma said brightly, "There was a snowflake! The first snowflake. That means it's officially winter now. We all tried to catch the snowflake on our tongues so we would get all the Christmas presents we want."

As far as Grogan was aware, the local legend promised the catcher of the first snowflake simply good luck for the duration of the season, but she declined to argue the point.

"Then," Emma went on, "I heard someone crying—well, not crying, but close to crying."

"You mean, whimpering?"

"Yeah, whimpering. I looked into the trees and I saw someone fall over. I went to go help her, but she was...well, I thought she was dead. She looked really dead. She was bloody and dirty. She wasn't breathing. And her eyes were, like, staring open—I think. It was hard to see because of her hair."

Grogan frowned. She squatted down before Emma. "Her hair?"

"Yeah, she had long, dark hair covering her eyes."

"And a jacket?"

12

"Uh-huh, a dark blue jacket. I think it's the kind where you can roll up the hood and put it inside the collar, because the collar had a zipper."

"And pants?"

"Khakis. They were really muddy."

"And her shoes?"

"Um, I didn't notice her shoes."

Oh my god...

Grogan straightened up. "That's...that's really good remembering, Emma. Thank you."

From the look he gave her, Frank Thurmin had caught on that something was up, but Grogan ignored him and ran to the sheriff, just then signing off. "I couldn't get hold of Deputy Tan," he said, "but Hayden, Trent, Powell, and Ziegler will be here in a few minutes. Tan can meet us once she gets the message. Megan couldn't have gotten far. It shouldn't take us long to find her."

"Keith, we have a problem. Some of the deputies should stay and keep searching Wenskee Woods."

"What are you talking about?"

"Megan was last seen wearing a yellow jacket, black jeans, and bright pink shoes, and she has very short hair."

"And?"

"Emma just gave me a description of the person she found. It doesn't match at all."

The sheriff frowned. "How is that possible? Unless..."

Grogan shrugged and nodded. "Unless I was right, and we have *two* missing girls."

* * *

"Once again, for those just joining us," boomed the voice of a basso profundo from radios throughout Veil, *"the sheriff's*

13

department has issued an amber alert for Megan Toombs, age eleven, last seen wearing a yellow jacket, pink shoes, and carrying a purple backpack. Excuse me, a lavender backpack. If anyone has information about her whereabouts, please contact the sheriff's department. She was reported missing at eleven-thirty today. The last people to see her said she was taking a short cut home from school through Wenskee Woods, where the sheriff and his deputies are conducting a search—wait... Uh, one moment, please." A pregnant silence followed. Listeners everywhere paused what they were doing, intrigued.

One pair of listeners was in an office, waiting for the return of the newscaster's voice. One of them was a tall, brawny man in his early forties, sitting with his goateed chin in his hand. He had the look of one who had started out anxious but was now bored. The placard on his desk identified him as Kurt Riner, an attorney. The woman, about the same age, her face and hair heavily made up, had been pacing for several minutes now. "What's going on?" she murmured. "Why hasn't he called?"

"He'll call," the man said almost absently.

The woman shook her head. "I don't like this, Kurt. Pressler will find a way to use this to his advantage—you know he will. We need to prepare. We need to have a game plan. We need to know what's going on—"

"Amy, will you stop wearing a hole in the carpet?"

"What carpet? It's a hardwood floor!"

"I know, it's just an expr—"

An abrupt clearing of the throat signaled the return of the newscaster. *"Sorry for the delay. We're getting a new report that the search for Megan Toombs has been diverted to a wooded area on the opposite side of town. Sources say the sheriff has located a witness who sighted—what?!"* The newscaster sounded agitated.

In one of the expensive houses on the mountainside, another listener looked over at the radio from where he was in the middle of a treadmill workout. The electronic speaker emitted some incoherent mutterings, then the newscaster was back once more. *"Again, my apologies. We now have a revised report. The sheriff's department is splitting their search between the two locations—Wenskee Woods and the wooded area adjacent to Mountain Boulevard. It was thought that a witness had spotted Megan in the latter area, but that sighting proved to be inaccurate, so it's not clear why they're still sending deputies there..."*

The man on the treadmill threw back his head and laughed. He laughed so hard he had to step off the machine.

"It could be we don't have all the pertinent information as yet, so please stay tuned and we'll keep you updated. Now, Mary DePalma with the weather."

The exercise room door opened and another man leaned in. He was younger, and he wore glasses. "Did you call me, Mr. Pressler?"

Pressler leaned on the treadmill, still chortling. "No, I didn't, Ernie, but I'm glad you're here. I need you for something." He turned off the machine and began to towel the sweat off his face. "I need an announcement put on all my social media pages. Get a hold of my contact at the radio station, too. Tell everyone to pass the message on to all their friends and neighbors."

"What message, sir?"

"To meet in the square at 3 p.m. sharp." He took a swig from a water bottle.

"Sir, I thought you'd decided not to hold any more impromptu campaign rallies."

"*Not* a campaign rally," Pressler said sharply. "Nothing to do with my campaign *whatsoever*."

"Yes, sir, I understand."

Pressler's lips curled into a wolfish smile. "Officially."

Ernie nodded. "What should I say is the purpose of the… gathering?"

Pressler paused on the threshold of his shower room. "Haven't you been listening, Ernie? We have a missing girl to find." He winked and went inside.

* * *

There was one person in Veil who, for the moment, was not following the narrative of Megan's disappearance as closely as everyone else.

Unlike the patch of forest Emma and her friends had found so frightening and claustrophobic, other parts were more spacious, inviting. These were the areas townspeople had explored more fully over the years, gradually forming natural paths, some of which became official trails with markers and LED lampposts. One post had a sign attached, warning trail-goers not to diverge from the path, citing a dangerous ravine nearby.

As an autumn breeze wafted through the forest, a pair of legs in jeans dangled lazily over the ravine.

Ding.

Sixteen-year-old Cyanne Grogan deflated. The sign warning people away had promised her some peaceful isolation, but her phone wouldn't stop making noise. First it had been the amber alert—some kid had gone missing. Probably an over-protective parent freaking out over nothing. Then her mother had called her, most likely wanting to make sure Cy was safe (not that there was any logical connection between a random girl's disappearance and Cy's safety). Cy knew that she'd get an earful for not answering, but she let it go to voicemail anyway.

16

She felt no compunction to give her mother peace of mind.

Ding.

The girl groaned in aggravation. Her mother could be quite persistent. Cy had lost count of how many text alerts had sounded. Maybe that would finally be the last one. Turning the phone off hardly seemed worth the effort—

Ding.

Cy reached over and pulled her phone out of her backpack sitting nearby. Items had shifted inside, so she pulled it out with the screen facing away from her. In turning it, one-handed, she lost her grip on the phone slightly and it started to fall from her grasp—straight into the ravine. She flung out her other hand to catch it—and in so doing, pushed herself marginally forward. She felt the edge of the ground beneath her thighs give ever so slightly. Bits of crumbled rock and dirt sprinkled out from under her legs and rained down past her ankles.

It was as if something inside of her that had been asleep suddenly awoke. With a yelp she rolled back, lifted her knees, and kicked down at the ground, at first only scuffing the ravine's edge but then managing to plant her heels in the earth and push herself back and away. She scrambled to her feet, her breath coming a mile a minute, her heart thumping hard against her ribs.

For a moment she stood there, catching her breath, gaping at the deep, empty space she'd been staring into so languidly a moment before. Then she jumped as the phone rang, and this time she did drop it. As she picked it up, she saw the screen and realized it wasn't her mother after all.

"H-hey, Azura."

"Hi, sis! Did you get my photos?"

"Photos?"

"Yeah, I just sent you a bunch."

"Oh…hang on." Cy went through her texts and discovered photos of her sister and other twenty-somethings carving Styrofoam pumpkins, followed by the results sitting outside, gradually getting buried in snow. There was also a decorative witch dummy whose arms had been arranged to wrap around herself, as if she were shivering in the cold. "They're cute," Cy said into the phone. Her voice was toneless, hollow.

"You okay? You sound weird."

"Yeah, I'm fine."

"Are you at home?"

"Yeah. No, I'm, I'm—I'm nowhere. Just walking through town."

"You might want to tell Mom that. She called me a little while ago. She's pretty worried that you didn't answer when she called you. You don't want her to ground you—again."

Cy thought briefly about tossing the phone into the ravine. Instead, in a low voice she said, "I don't care."

Azura laughed. *"I remember when you were the grown-up and I was the rebel. I guess we switched."* Was she teasing her? Or was she trying to start a conversation through nostalgia?

All Cy said in response was, "Yeah."

Part of her wanted to talk to Azura—or anyone, really. To express her feelings like a normal person. To be listened to. To be hopeful that she might eventually not feel so miserable. *To tell someone what happened with Rob,* thought a deeper part of her. The problem was, if she felt better, then her *mother* would feel better, too. At the thought of that, her blood boiled.

Azura seemed to sense that no actual conversation was forthcoming. *"Well, glad you're…okay,"* she said with a hint of doubt. *"You can always call me, or email me if reception's bad."*

Cy knew this already. "Okay," she said.

Azura sighed. *"Okay. I hope they find your friend."*

Cy blinked. "My friend?"

"Yeah, the one who's missing."

"I don't"—*have any friends here,* she finished mentally—"know who it is that's missing."

"Um, Mom said it was a girl named Megan?"

"Megan…"

"Yeah, Megan Toombs, I think."

Cy made an involuntary jolt. *"That's* who's missing?"

"So she is *your friend."* Azura sounded almost as surprised as Cy.

Cy thought about the time she babysat Megan back in August, remembered how the eleven-year-old, believing she was far too old for a babysitter, at first showed resentment toward Cy and anger at her over-protective mother. Cy remembered how she'd eventually won Megan's approval by favoring the right kinds of music (and showing disdain for the wrong kinds). To their mutual surprise, the two of them had had fun together, and Cy had developed a fondness for Megan—especially after the girl told of her parents' divorce. They had admitted to each other brief moments when they'd considered running away from home. Had Megan taken it a step further?

"Cy? Are you there?"

"I—I gotta go."

"Cy, are you okay?"

"I have to go, I love you, bye!" Cy hung up, wheeled about, seized her bag, and ran back along the trail to its entrance. There she picked up her bike from where it leaned against a tree and pedaled away at a breakneck pace.

II

ow...what was I doing?

N In the immediate sense, the person who had this thought was pushing coniferous tree branches out of her face as she struggled forward. The trees were close all around her, pressing in, the branches sticky with sap—was it sap? She glanced at her palm. Nope, that was bird poop. It was all over her, covering what wasn't already slathered in mud and tiny wood chips and fragments of leaves and...and...what was the stuff on her head? Oh, right, blood. Yes, she'd discovered that when she'd woken up in the mud.

No...not in the mud. On the grass. Beside a road.

Or beside a river...

One of those. It was right after she'd opened her eyes and seen the little cute blond girl standing over her.

Or before.

No, it was definitely after, because she remembered sitting up and feeling the wetness on her forehead. Her fingers came away red when she touched it, and after the girl went away, she found her fingers already stained red, so it was definitely...

...before.

Wait, what was before? Why was she having such a problem remembering things?

No, no, it wasn't that she couldn't remember. Of course she could remember. Why couldn't she remember?

But she *did* remember. She remembered remembering just a moment ago. The trees, the mud, the bird poop, the blood, the girl—

The girl! That was it! She'd seen the girl, tried to speak to her but couldn't, and then the girl was gone, so she went after her as fast as she could.

Because…?

She groaned. Trying to keep things straight in her head was as aggravating as getting through these *god—damn—BRANCHES!* She swung her arms forcefully, sweeping the boughs aside harder and harder, though every third one tended to slip past her arm, whipping her in the face and the chest.

Why was she following the girl? There was something she was missing, something she'd forgotten that she shouldn't have, something extremely obvious…

In the next second, she tripped on a rock and fell. Suddenly it came to her—what she'd forgotten—why she was having such trouble remembering—

Pain!!! Pain so intense it impeded her awareness of it. Pain *everywhere*, in her arms, her chest, her hips, her feet, her head—oh, her *head*—like her crown was trying to unscrew itself from her skull, made all the worse by the pounding, booming noise, that noise that just wouldn't stop, so loud she couldn't even *hear* it (and she lacked the energy to even try to make sense of that).

As bad as the pain was, even worse was the confusion. The inability to keep her focus and attention, intensified by her agony, left her fully aware of only one thing: how vulnerable she was. Vulnerable and alone.

She threw back her head and screamed. It was a wail of raw agony, rage, and pleading. But no one came to help.

Help—yes, *that was it!* A small part of her rejoiced as she finally remembered—*that* was why she was following the girl. Where there were children, adults couldn't be too far off. And it had only been a second ago that she'd seen the kid.

Was it a second ago...or an hour? Clarity flickered. Despair returned. If she hadn't found help yet, then she must have gone in the wrong direction. She was lost, injured, and quickly losing her faculties. She clutched her head with one hand and hugged herself with the other, and sobbed.

Eventually she got wobbly to her feet and pressed on. She had to keep trying to find help. At the very least, she had to get out of these trees. That way, if she fell or lost consciousness, there was a greater chance that someone would find her—

All at once, she pushed past another set of branches and there were no more trees. For an instant, she felt jubilation.

The problem was, there was no more ground either.

She pitched forward down the steep embankment, headlong into the river. She was quickly submerged, and she thrust her head up to gulp in some air—except up and down seemed to have exchanged places. She thrashed and contorted, finally getting her head past the water's surface and hacking, spewing water from her lungs.

If the rapids had been severe, she might never have made it out. It was a frightening few minutes, but with a little bit of frantic flailing and clawing, she reached the far side of the river and hauled herself onto dry grass. She shivered, feeling the damp cold permeate her skin and chill her insides, but the cold seemed to dull some of her pain, for which she was grateful.

Except, she realized as she lay on her back in the grass,

she really wasn't in that much pain to begin with. No, that wasn't true, there were aches and pains throughout her body. But that all-consuming agony that kept distracting her in the forest, disorienting her...that wasn't real. The dunking in the river seemed to have shaken her discombobulated thoughts and senses and brought them back into something resembling normalcy. She could remember the past hour, trace back through her memories, even if some of them flickered in and out—probably spots where she'd briefly lost consciousness. She could tell, now, that the pain she thought she was experiencing was not actually real.

But wait, no—it *was* real! She was *sure* of that. The pain had definitely been real, so what...how...?

She squeezed her eyes shut. *Focus.*

In time, the answer came to her. The memory of the pain was, indeed, real. In her semi-conscious state, the memory of that pain had become so vivid that it had incapacitated her, made her *think* it was happening in the present. Even now, the thought of it made her want to wretch...but she controlled the feeling, pushed it back so it wasn't overwhelming her, put it in perspective.

What had caused such debilitating pain? What had happened? She cast her mind back...but it was like trying to look back along a road as one drove onward. Past a certain point on the horizon, always receding, the road became invisible. She remembered stumbling along in the forest, remembered the cute little girl, but everything else was just too far back to see clearly. Whatever incident had caused the pain must have happened before that, an event so intense that when she thought of it, it was like feeling the pain all over again. It was the same with the noise. There had been no noise in the forest, but a noise *had* occurred, so loud and so frightening that the memory was indistinguishable from the sensation, making it seem like it was *still* happening—until now. Her unintended swim might be freezing her to death, but at least she could *think*.

She rolled over, her backside taking a turn in the chilling air while her front enjoyed the relief of paltry warmth. If she remained lying here, she might get hypothermia. That thought was disturbing enough, but it occurred to her that the symptoms of hypothermia included intense confusion and disorientation. Fearing a return to her mental state from before, she found the motivation to get to her feet. It took her a couple tries, what with dizziness and cold making her shiver uncontrollably. She blinked several times to try to get her vision back into focus. Finally she was standing, her body and her mind sufficiently (if not optimally) intact, and she took a step forward.

Her face hit something and she fell back down.

"What the...?" Even with her vision still adjusting, she could have sworn there was nothing in front of her face.

She pushed herself up again—and the top of her head hit something. She reached up—yes, there was definitely a solid object there. Why couldn't she see it? It was long and thin, taut, corded. She felt with her other hand; there were more cords, knotted together. This was some sort of web, held in place somehow.

She brought her face up to it, blinked, squinted, blinked again, and finally the image resolved itself: it wasn't a web. It was a net. She stepped back, saw the two posts holding it up on either side. A volleyball net.

She saw a structure nearby, and ducked underneath the net to investigate. It was a roof held up by stone pillars, with picnic tables underneath. On one of the seats were the words, *Property of Riverbend Park*.

She turned on the spot and saw, now that her vision was nearly restored, the river curving around the park in a U-shape. Here and there, on the river's edge, were more picnic tables overlooking the water. Just over the hill she could see the top of a batting cage, and to the side, a sign with an arrow directing visitors to the Veil Hockey Pavilion.

Veil. Was that a person, or a place?

There might be people at the pavilion. At long last, she could find some help. She started in that direction.

"Megan?" said a voice.

A deep, paralyzing dread seized her in an unrelenting grip. Whoever had spoken was on the other side of the pillar. All she had to do was step out from behind it and ask for help, but an overwhelming instinct kept her from moving.

"Megan, are you here? It's me, Cy." It was a girl's voice. A teenage girl. Footsteps cracked along the stone floor beneath the structure.

She tried to fight the instinct to hide. She was hurt, she desperately needed medical attention... Why couldn't she move???

It took all her effort to peep out from behind the pillar. She saw a teenager, about sixteen, with long, chestnut brown hair and bright blue eyes.

"Megan, if you're here, I just want to talk to you. Or you can do the talking, if you want. I can listen." The girl stepped out from beneath the structure and stared searchingly across the expansive lawn. From her expression, the girl was obviously worried. "Megan!!" she called. There was no answer.

This was getting ridiculous. She was shivering harder than

ever. It was a wonder the noise of her teeth chattering hadn't given her presence away. The girl, Cy (what an unusual name), was obviously no threat to her. Beyond the pillar, she heard the girl sigh, then heard shoes scraping along the ground as the girl turned to go. It had to be now, she had to speak up before the girl left. She summoned all her bravery, built up her determination to step out where she'd be seen—

A second set of footsteps sounded on the concrete floor. The girl gave a frightened gasp.

* * *

"R-Rob?"

"Aw, sorry. I didn't mean to scare you." The tall, lean nineteen-year-old chuckled, his teeth showing. Behind his glasses, his eyes didn't look sorry at all.

Cy tried to keep her voice from trembling. "What are you doing here?"

With a casual air, Rob picked up a football lying discarded in the grass and began tossing it from one hand to the other. "Well, I was at the radio station and I saw you go by on your bike. You looked worried." He set the football atop a metal post and spun it. "Then I remembered—you're friends with Megan, aren't you? The girl who's missing. I thought, maybe you know where she is. So I caught up with you. Would make a good story if you found her."

Cy narrowed her eyes. "You followed me."

"Come on, don't start that again." Anyone who knew him less well would've missed the threatening edge that crept into his voice. "You know I'm an intern at the newspaper. The sooner I break a big story, the less I have to wait for them to make me a real reporter. And you know I hate waiting." That chuckle again. It always came when he was being ominous or menacing, as if to say, reassuringly, that he wasn't really. She knew, now, that chuckle was a lie.

Cy felt something touch her waist, and with a start she realized it was Rob's hand—how had she not noticed him moving closer? "Don't!" she cried, springing away from him. "Don't touch me." She tried to sound tough, but failed to keep her voice from quavering. Gathering her courage, she snapped, "You *were* following me, Rob. Not from the radio station, but from the ravine trail, and maybe even before that."

Rob scoffed. "What are you talking about?"

"You have yellow leaves on the back of your jacket."

Rob craned his neck to look. "Uh, yes, there are leaves on me. That's something that happens in autumn," he said in an are-you-stupid tone of voice.

Cy cursed her voice as it trembled. "They're *yellow* leaves. Around town the leaves are only red and orange. But they're yellow on the ravine trail. You looked for me there, but you couldn't find me 'cause I went off the trail. You saw me come out and you followed me here. You're stalking me—again."

"No, come on! I never stalked you, okay? I explained that." He chuckled again. "It's cute how you keep having the same thought even after you're proven wrong."

"You're trying to mess with me, but I know it's true."

He paused, and then, his veneer of friendliness dissolving: "Yeah, well, there are some things you *don't* know."

"I'm leaving," said Cy, walking in a wide circle around him. She wasn't about to let him back into her head.

"Like things about your dad."

She stopped dead. "What did you say?"

"Your mom didn't tell you the truth about him. About his death."

27

"What are you talking about?"

"You want me to tell you?" He approached her again. She could feel the very skin on her bones shrink away from him. "First let's get one thing straight: you're not gonna tell your mom we talked. Just 'cause your mom's a deputy, you can't use her to get back at me when your feelings are hurt."

"That's not what I—"

"Yes, it is. You told her I was mistreating you."

Cy gulped. "You...you did."

Rob affected a disappointed tone. "Why do you have to be like that? You don't have any friends here in Veil, but *I* went out with you. I was nice to you. Maybe we had a few fights, but I know you still like me. The only thing you *didn't* like is that when we fought, I didn't just let you win. I'm not that kind of guy. I shouldn't have to pretend you're right when you're not. *You* can pretend all you want, but deep down, you know it's true. So let's stop pretending...and maybe then I'll tell you the truth about your dad."

Cy shook her head firmly. "I'm not going out with you again."

"Well, I mean, we don't have to go out. Not officially."

Cy blanched. "Forget it."

She didn't think he was close enough to catch her if she ran. She was wrong. His large hand clamped iron-hard around her arm. "Now, come on!" he snarled. "I can tell you want to!"

"Let go of me!"

"Just wait a minute—"

"*Help!*"

"Stop that!" His hands seemed to be everywhere at once, covering her mouth, immobilizing her. She was no match for him, and he had her here all alone...

"*Let her go!!!*"

They were both so startled they froze in place. In the next instant, Cy took advantage of Rob's distraction and twisted free of him.

The voice that had shouted—or croaked, more like—was hoarse, raspy, but chilling in its tone of command—and warning. Halloween wasn't too far off, so in her head Cy imagined, briefly, a green-skinned hag with warts.

"Who's that?" Rob spat. Cy couldn't tell where the voice had come from, but Rob apparently thought it had come from behind the nearest pillar, for he edged toward it. "Who is that?!"

All at once something sprang out from behind the pillar—something ugly, dripping mud and goo. It raised its arms and screeched in his face.

Rob cried out and nearly fell over. He scurried away and up the hill, barely glancing back before he dropped down the other side.

Cy stood there, stunned, torn between the sight of Rob fleeing and the newcomer. Looking at her more closely, she could see it was a small woman, soaking wet and covered in…well, all sorts of things. She was also bleeding from her head. Suddenly the woman sagged, exhausted, and Cy shot forward to catch and support her, not minding the muck and grime.

The woman tried to speak. "Hosp…"

"Hos—oh, hospital! Yeah, okay!" Cy helped her to one of the picnic table seats and took out her cell phone. As she made the call, she said, "Who are you? What's your name?"

The woman stared at her a moment, then said matter-of-factly, "I don't know."

29

III

"*Hello?*"

"It's me."

"*Cy! Wait, I recognize this number—why are you at the hospital?!*"

"Mom, calm down, I'm fine. I found this girl at Riverbend Park. She was injured and I called nine-one-one. Then my phone died, so I had to use this one at the reception desk."

"*You went to the hospital with this girl?*"

"Well, um, yeah."

"*That...was very nice of you. I was upset you didn't call me back earlier, but it sounds like you were occupied, doing something good. I'm proud of you.*"

"Er..."

"*Has her family been contacted?*"

"I don't think so. They couldn't find any ID on her, and she said she doesn't remember who she is."

"*You mean she has amnesia?!*"

"I guess."

"*Wait, did you say Riverbend Park?*"

"Yeah."

"*That's close to—what was this girl wearing?*"

"Uh, dark blue jacket, khakis, and black-and-white Converse."

30

"And her hair is dark?"

"Y-yeah…"

"Sheriff! Cy, I have to go. I'll meet you at the hospital, okay?"

"Wait, but Mom—"

"I love you!"

"Mom, I left my bike at the—hello?"

* * *

If Sheriff Dubowski's head had been in fewer places, he would've had the presence of mind not to take the phone call. Between organizing the search near the school, then tightening the search to concentrate on the area where Emma Thurmin had found the "dead body," followed by Deputy Grogan's discovery that the body, dead or otherwise, was not the missing Megan but yet another lost girl (so far unreported) and having to reorganize the search all over again, and through it all supplying the distraught parents with token reassurances, his mental faculties were starting to wear thin. Now Grogan's daughter had discovered some girl who matched the description of the person Emma had found, which meant at last they could—again—focus their efforts on the original search area.

Grogan was on her way to the hospital. Dubowski and the other deputies who had been searching the woods by Mountain Boulevard were about to rejoin the rest at Wenskee Woods. The sheriff had just opened the door of his patrol car when his cell phone rang. He answered, "Dubowski."

"Keith," said a woman's voice, *"what the hell is going on? Did a kid find Megan Toombs's body in the woods or not?"*

The sheriff looked at the screen of his phone incredulously, registering (too late) the phone number. Ducking into his car and shutting the door, he hissed, "Are you crazy?! We can't be in contact over this! If someone found out—"

"Pressler's gathering half the town in the square this afternoon! He's going to start his own search for the girl. He's trying to destroy confidence in the sheriff's department—in you!*"*

"Amy, think it through. It'll be destroyed even more if people find out that we—"

"I told you you shouldn't have made public your support for Kurt too soon! Now, if someone in Pressler's search party finds the girl first, it'll hurt our campaign! We need to gauge a careful public response. We need information!"

"Not from me." The sheriff bit off each word.

"Don't you hang up on me!" snapped the woman, but that is exactly what the sheriff did, and he turned off his phone for good measure.

He jumped at the sound of someone knocking on his window. "Everything all right, Sheriff?" asked Deputy Derrick once the window was rolled down.

"Yes," said the sheriff, roughly tossing the phone into the seat beside him. At Derrick's look of concern, he jerked his thumb at the phone and said, "Calorie counting app."

"Oh, I see. Sheriff, there's something you should know. Elijah Pressler's organizing his own search for Megan Toombs."

Dubowski sighed with closed eyes. "Well, good for Pressler. A restless town like this, he'll help folks burn off some excess energy, give people some excitement." He moved to start his ignition.

"Sir," said Derrick, "don't you think you should be there?"

"Where?"

"In the square, when he gets everyone together."

"What for?"

"To tell him to stop, to tell them all to go home and let the sheriff's department handle this. Don't you think he's trying to

32

show us up, make us look incompetent—to get back at you for supporting his opponent in the election?"

"You know what, Deputy?" the sheriff said with exaggerated patience. "I think that's exactly what he's trying to do. I think it's obvious—so obvious that it's not going to work. It's going to backfire, and more people will see him for the charlatan he is. As long as he doesn't get in our way, there's no reason for us to stop him from doing something that's not illegal."

"But what if one of his people finds the girl before we do?!"

The sheriff turned and leveled a hard stare at the younger man. Derrick drew back, but the sheriff laid his hand on the deputy's shoulder, digging his fingers in. "Then she'll be back with her parents even sooner, and we'll *all* be happy," he said quietly.

Deputy Derrick's eyes went down as he nodded. "Yes, sir."

Satisfied, the sheriff sent the deputy on his way. Once again, he was just about to start his ignition when his radio blared to life. Dispatch was calling him. Suppressing a groan, he answered. Dispatch gave him a message.

Sheriff Dubowski sat, stunned, for a moment. Then he had dispatch repeat the message. When he'd finally processed what he'd been told, he did groan.

* * *

"Are you feeling all right?"

The woman jumped—or would have if she weren't lying on her back in a hospital bed. She'd been concentrating, straining, trying to remember...anything. Anything that had happened before that harrowing journey through the forest. What had caused her injuries? What had made that loud noise? What was her *name?!* Nothing came to her. It was as if she'd popped into existence all of a sudden, with nothing but instinct and a command of the English language. Now that all the mud and filth had been washed away, she'd spent the last few minutes acquainting herself with limbs, head, and torso. She turned her hands over before her eyes, examining her palms, her knuckles, noticing the way her right wrist made a slight clicking sound when she twisted it. She experimented, bending and turning each joint, running her fingers over her arms, her chest, her face, hair, and neck.

Rather than answer Cy's question, she stared at her in some surprise and said, "You're still here?"

Cy shrugged. "My house is too far to walk. I just called my mom for a ride."

The woman nodded. "Right. Your bike."

"What?"

"I said, your bike. I remember you were in the ambulance with me, so you must've left your bike at the park."

"How did you know I had a bike?"

"Your…ex mentioned it."

"Oh, right." Cy looked down.

"All those things he said to you… He's—horrible."

"Thanks." Cy let out a giggle. "You scared him good."

For a moment they shared the laughter.

Cy sat next to her on the bed. "So, have you remembered your name or anything about your life?"

The woman sighed and shook her head in discouragement.

"I can't imagine what it's like, not being able to remember your identity."

"I guess it's like…starting a book right in the middle. You don't know what's going on, but somehow you're part of the story."

"Well, what did the doctors say about it?"

"They said there's no set treatment for amnesia. They're going to call social services. Hopefully someone in town knows me, so even if I don't get my memories back, they can…" She trailed off, realizing she wasn't at all sure what was going to happen. Then she looked over at Cy and saw how concerned she was. "Look," she said, "try not to worry about me. I… I might've died if not for you. I was scared and alone and covered in blood and dirt, and now I'm all clean, lying in this bed, listening to Nelly Furtado on the radio."

Cy let out a laugh. She hadn't even noticed the low-volume radio music playing in the background.

"The point is, whatever happens, I'm going to be okay. You saved my life."

In a low voice, Cy said, "You kinda saved me, too."

"Well, then, we're even. You don't have to stay and watch over me. Go home. Call a friend. Don't let me keep you away from your life."

Cy inhaled deeply, let it out, and nodded. "Okay."

"Tell you what. Write down your name and number for me. I'll call you once I find out I'm a millionaire heiress. I'll buy you a boat or something."

Cy took some paper out of her backpack and wrote down her name and phone number. Then she swung her bag over her shoulder and moved toward the door. At the threshold, she stopped and looked back.

Her new friend waved the piece of paper and quipped, "I've memorized it already."

Cy nodded, smiling, and went out the door.

Her friend's cheerful mood sank like a stone. She stared glumly out the window and took a deep, unsteady breath.

Then Cy reappeared. "Hey, um…just wanted to make sure—

you know where you are, don't you?"

"Uh…Veil," said her friend.

There was a pause. "In Vermont," said Cy.

"Vermont, yes. That explains the mountains." She made a half-hearted gesture toward the window.

Cy nodded again and once more moved as if to exit, but then hesitated. "Hey, can we just try something?"

"Try what?"

Cy came back and sat next to her, took out another piece of paper and a hardcover textbook, and set them on her friend's lap, along with a pencil. "Write the words, 'My name is,' and then…see what your hand does next."

"You're thinking of muscle memory?"

Cy shrugged. "It's worth a try."

Her friend hesitated, then picked up the pencil. She frowned, then used her other hand to adjust the pencil between her fingers. It took a few tries before she found a position that felt right. Then, after another deep breath, she touched the pencil-point to the paper and wrote a capital M. She wrote each line of the letter with a separate, mechanical stroke. She scowled, then scribbled that out.

Taking a breath and willing her hand to relax, she said, "My name is…" and began to write. On the paper appeared a beautiful cursive *M*, then a lower-case *y* with a loop at the end.

A grin broke out on Cy's face.

Her friend went on. Each letter looked like a work of art. When she reached the *s* in *is* they both held their breath…

But nothing happened. The pencil hovered over the empty space, trembling.

After ten seconds, she gave up. She dropped the pencil, which rolled off the textbook and onto the floor. "It was a good idea," she said shortly, hiding her dejection.

"At least we know you have good penmanship," said Cy.

"Yeah. And I know where Vermont is."

"And who Nelly Furtado is."

After a moment, they looked at each other. Cy scooped up the pencil and handed it back to her friend, who started scribbling down a list: *penmanship, Vermont, Nelly Furtado.*

The list continued to grow for several minutes, until a tapping made them look up. Standing in the doorway was a woman in her early forties, close to six feet tall, lean in face and body, her dirty blond hair pulled back in a ponytail and wearing an earthy-tan deputy's uniform. Her nose was long and thin, her eyes pale blue.

The woman in the bed knew, before anyone told her, that this woman and Cy were mother and daughter.

* * *

When Jen Grogan arrived at the hospital, she was shown to a recovery room, where she found her daughter sitting beside a young girl in a metal-framed bed.

Then she looked again. It wasn't a girl at all; it was an adult. A small adult, to be sure—she couldn't be taller than five feet, if that—but her features were decidedly not those of an adolescent. Jen could understand how Emma, unable to see her face clearly, had mistaken the body in the woods for that of a tween girl like Megan. She made a mental note to confirm the woman's age with the doctors treating her (who would clarify that the patient was between age twenty and twenty-five).

The hair that had obscured that face had been washed, along with the rest of the young woman's body, as the doctors had cleaned and dressed her wounds. Her hair was dark brown, with a streak of purple on one side, and her eyes were a shade of amber-yellow that Jen had never seen before. Just above the eyes was a nasty-looking gash on her forehead.

But what struck Jen the most was that her daughter Cyanne—the same girl who, for the last few months, had outright refused and avoided any and every activity that risked the slightest possibility of social interaction and development of human connection—was talking and laughing with this young woman as if they were old friends. Jen stared through the door, bewildered; a small corner of her heart felt joy and relief. This was a side of Cy she hadn't seen in a long time, a side of her that she'd missed.

The mask of Cy's usual closed-off self materialized the moment she saw her mother. The young woman in the bed seemed to notice the change in Cy's demeanor.

The deputy approached the bed and proffered a hand. "I'm Deputy Jen Grogan, Cy's mother."

The young woman shook it. "Nice to meet you," she said. "I'd tell you my name, but we haven't quite worked that out yet."

Jen saw Cy's calculus textbook sitting on the woman's lap, with a handwritten list on top of it. Jen had never encountered a case of amnesia, but she'd heard that while forgetting one's identity was a frequent plot device of movies and TV shows, it was a much rarer occurrence in real life. She didn't want Cy to invest herself in this person's situation only to find out she was a fraud. Was there a way to test whether or not this woman was lying?

All this went through her head in the second or two before she replied, "Your memories are still blocked?"

The young woman shrugged and gave a lopsided smile.

"She can remember a lot, actually," Cy put in. "Just not the

38

main stuff—about herself." She looked down the list. "She knows what year it is, she knows the state capitals, she knows the quadratic formula," at which point she lifted the calculus textbook, "she can remember that McDonalds and Burger King are restaurants—but doesn't specifically remember eating at either one—she knows *Sesame Street* is a TV show—but not whether she's actually seen it—a lot of stuff like that."

The young woman added, "I can also—apparently—remember all the words to the song 'Maneater' by Nelly Furtado…which I'm not sure I want to know the reason for."

Cy giggled.

"Can you remember anything about what happened in the woods?" asked Jen.

The young woman's mood became somber. "I…remember touching my forehead and finding blood there. I remember waking up, lying on my back—I must've blacked out—and this little blond girl found me. I tried to follow her, but I got lost. Next thing I knew, I was in the river. And then I met Cy."

Jen watched the young woman carefully. "Nothing earlier?"

The woman's eyes closed briefly in what looked like frustration, then she looked away, as if into the distance, straining, reaching…and then blowing out her breath in aggravation. "I've been trying," she said. Cy squeezed her shoulder.

Jen's eyes flicked up to the gash on the woman's forehead. "Do you think you were attacked?"

"I don't know," the woman said helplessly.

Jen nodded, admitting to herself that the woman's reaction seemed genuine. Then she turned to her daughter. "Cy, what were you doing at Riverbend Park?" she asked.

A quick look passed between Cy and the young woman, something furtive, which Jen didn't know how to interpret.

"I was looking for Megan," said Cy. "She once told me she goes there sometimes when she wants to be alone, when she's scared or upset. I guess you haven't found her yet?"

"No, honey, I'm sorry." To the young woman she said, "We have an eleven-year-old girl missing. We've been searching for her for hours. I'm afraid your case is going to have to take a backseat until we find her."

"I understand," the woman said wholeheartedly.

"The doctors told me they'd like to keep you overnight for observation, but tomorrow we can bring you to the station and take your fingerprints, see if anything comes up."

"You mean, like, if she's a criminal?" Cy looked indignant on the woman's behalf.

"Or a teacher," said the young woman. "Teachers have their fingerprints on file." After a moment of thought, she added another item to the list.

Just then Jen's radio sputtered to life. *"Grogan, come in,"* said the sheriff's voice. Jen retreated into the hall to make her reply.

"Hey. Thanks," Cy said softly to her friend.

"For what?"

"For not telling Mom about Rob."

The young woman tilted her head. "You're not going to?"

Cy frowned to herself.

Your mom didn't tell you the truth about him. About his death.

"I don't know yet," she mumbled.

Then with a quick shake of her head she asked, "So what are we going to call you?"

The woman gave her a blank look. "Excuse me?"

"I mean, until you get your memories back. What name should we call you?"

The woman shook her head slowly. "I have no idea."

A mischievous glint came into Cy's eye. "How about Nelly?"

The young woman made a face at her that was half amusement, half grimace.

"Or maybe Jane," suggested Cy.

"Why Jane?"

"As in Jane Doe."

"Like a corpse? I don't think so."

"Or Callie."

"Callie?"

"Short for cal…culus? Okay, no, that's dumb."

The woman gave a half-hearted laugh. Then with a tentative breath she said, "I'll give Nelly a try."

Cy held out a hand. "Welcome to Veil, Nelly."

"Thanks," Nelly said with a wry smile. Then, sobering, she said, "Seriously, though, I would think about telling your mom about what happened in the park."

Cy bit her lip and glanced toward the door.

A minute later, Cy came up to her mother in the hall. Jen was signing off on her radio. "Mom, can I talk to you?"

Her mother turned and Cy saw the pale, grave look on her face. "Mom? What is it?"

"There's new evidence. It looks like Megan might have been abducted," Jen said after a moment's hesitation.

"What new evidence?"

Jen shook her head firmly. "You know I can't tell you that, Cy."

"What if," Cy interrupted her, then paused, and with her voice lowered continued, "What if someone kidnapped Megan, and—and they were seen?"

"Seen?"

"Yeah." Cy pointed into the room behind her and whispered,

"By Nelly."

"Nelly? Who's Nelly?"

Forgetting to keep her voice down, Cy said, "That's what we're calling her now."

"Provisionally!" called a voice from the recovery room.

Jen saw where this was going. "Cy—"

"Nelly saw the kidnapping, and she tried to go for help," Cy insisted as she pulled her mother away from the door, out of earshot. "The kidnapper caught up with her and knocked her out!"

"Cy—"

"Maybe he thought she was dead, so he left her, but then she woke up and—"

"Cy, there's no evidence for any of that."

"I know, but...but what are the odds of an injury like that happening with no witnesses?" When Jen didn't have a ready answer for that, Cy went on, "And if there *was* a witness and they haven't come forward, that means someone's keeping a secret. And if someone's keeping a secret like that on the same day as a kidnapping, and they're not connected...that's a *really* big coincidence."

Jen gave a sigh, but there was amusement in it. "Even if you're right, Cy, what can we do? Nelly can't remember anything."

"She said a little blond girl found her! If we find the girl—"

"That was Emma Thurmin. She saw Nelly in the woods near Mountain Boulevard."

"Then that's where Nelly lost her—"

"No, her clothes were already filthy. She'd been trekking through the woods long before that, but even the sheriff can't tell where from. And neither can she."

"I can help her remember!"

"Sweetie…"

"Did you see how long that list was? The list of stuff she's remembered? That came from just fifteen minutes of me sitting with her. If I could show her around Veil—"

"The doctors want to keep her in the hospital."

"For observation! That means she's fine physically."

"She has a concussion."

"A *mild* concussion. She's fine to get out of bed as long as she doesn't over-exert herself."

Jen took a deep breath and let it out slowly. The truth was, she found herself liking the young woman with no memory. She wanted to help her, to give her case the attention it deserved. That just wasn't possible right now.

And what about Cy? After months of putting up with her moping, seeing her want so badly to be involved in something important was an absolute miracle. (And this was the most Cy had spoken to her in a single conversation in recent weeks.) How could Jen say no? After all, it was just possible Cy was onto something.

Apparently Jen needed to work on her poker face, because her expression made Cy break into a wide grin. In as stern a voice as she could manage, Jen said, "I'll see if the hospital has any spare clothes Nelly can wear, then I'll check with the sheriff and see if we can get her released into our department's custody. With the search turning into an investigation, maybe we can spare a deputy to escort you two."

Cy dove back into the hospital room to give her friend the news. A moment later, she stuck her head out again and said, "Thanks, Mom!" before she ducked back in and shut the door.

Jen's breath caught for a second before she turned to go speak to the doctors. For a moment, just before Cy had moved toward the door, it had seemed she was about to hug her mother. If she had, it would've been the first hug they'd shared since before Jen had told her of her father's death.

IV

Beneath the bandage covering most of her forehead, Nelly's eyes were glued to the backseat window as the patrol car drove down Veil's Main Street. She took in every building they passed: the post office, the library, the movie theater, the restaurants, the banks, the bowling alley—nearly all of which featured one sort of Halloween decoration or another. She observed the lampposts lining the street, bats and large spiders hanging from some. Townspeople strolled up and down the sidewalks, kicking and stirring up red and orange leaves scattered along the pavement.

"Anything familiar to you?" said a voice.

Nelly looked at the driver, a short-haired African-American man in his early twenties wearing a deputy's uniform. "Not yet," she replied. "But the town looks nice. Everything's so clean, friendly-feeling."

The driver nodded. "It's not bad," he said, "as small towns go."

She had met this man outside the hospital shortly after changing into the clothes provided by the doctors (a long-sleeve shirt with a mountain graphic, a denim jacket, a pair of jeans, and boot-like shoes that were clearly suited for colder, wetter weather). Cy had introduced the man as Deputy Benno. "He's the rookie deputy," she'd said.

Benno had made a face at her. "I've been with the department for over a year."

"Yeah, but there have been no new deputies since you started—other than my mom, but she's the *senior* deputy—so technically you're still the rookie."

"Calling me a rookie makes me sound like a red shirt."

"You mean like in *Star Trek*?" Nelly had asked.

"Exactly. I'd prefer to survive past the first commercial, thank you."

Nelly had quickly jotted the words *Star Trek* on her list as Benno held the door for her.

Now, in the car, Cy pointed out her own window, directing Nelly's attention to a cross-street. "That's Mountain Boulevard, where Mom said that girl, Emma, found you."

The patrol car moved through the intersection. Nelly asked, "Are we not going down there?"

"Well, your clothes were already dirty by the time Emma saw you, so you probably came from somewhere else." Cy pulled a brochure from her backpack that Nelly had seen her take from the hospital lobby. She opened it, revealing a map of Veil. "Here are the woods by Mountain Boulevard, and here's Riverbend Park. If you draw a line through," she said, tracing a line with her finger from the park to the woods and further on, "then you end up in this area."

"What's there?"

"Well, this old building here used to be the grocery store, but it's abandoned now. If you keep on going, you get to Platte."

"Platte?"

"It's sort of a suburb; it's technically not part of the town, but it's only a mile or so outside the town limits. There's a café, a gas station, some houses, and the old ice rink."

Nelly shook her head doubtfully. "Platte connects to Veil by highway," she pointed out, "and it looks like it's all grass and fields around that area. I might have been out of it, but I'm pretty sure I'd have chosen to head for the highway rather than diving into a forest and getting lost." *Unless I needed to run away from something,* she thought as into her mind flashed the memory of hearing Cy's voice for the first time, and how her first instinct was to hide.

"Well," said Cy, "there's a farmer's market going on in the parking lot of the old grocery store, and it's been there since this morning. Maybe someone there saw you. Or if you're a local, there's a chance someone there might know you."

Nelly didn't have any better ideas.

The patrol car slowed as multiple pedestrians crossed the street toward a large grassy park, where dozens of people were massing in the center. "This is the village square," said Cy. "I don't know why all these people are here."

"Those are Pressler's searchers," said Deputy Benno.

"Pressler?" Nelly asked.

"Elijah Pressler. Owns property all over town. He's gathering volunteers to help search for Megan."

"That's good, isn't it?" asked Cy.

"Sure," Benno said with a heavy lack of enthusiasm.

Cy noticed Nelly craning her neck to stare at the locals in the square. "Are any of them familiar?" she asked her.

Nelly sighed and gave Cy a wry smile. "That's what I keep asking myself. Do I know this person, this place? Did something important happen to me here? Am I in love with someone?" She drew an unsteady breath. "Even if I find out who I am, what if I still can't remember? What if I find out I had a great life, and now I've lost it?"

Cy didn't know what to say. She squeezed Nelly's hand.

A few minutes later, they reached the farmer's market. The vendors were beginning to close up shop. Just before they got out of the patrol car, Nelly hesitated. "So…how does this work? Do I just walk around and hope someone notices me who knows me and says, 'Hello…Zelda'?"

"I was thinking—if you're comfortable with it—I'll just take you to each vendor and ask them if they recognize you," said Cy.

Nelly said it sounded like a plan.

"I know exactly the person you should start with," said Deputy Benno. "Come with me." He led them to a stall where two elderly women in woolen sweaters were loading multiple baskets of apples into a van parked nearby. Nelly had to stop and tie one of her shoes, which took her a minute or two because her fingers were still sore. Cy waited with her, and watched as Benno went up to one of the women and tapped her on the shoulder. Upon seeing Benno, the woman's face lit up with a wide smile, but she didn't speak. Instead she moved her hands in a complicated pattern of movements. Benno answered in kind. They were signing, Cy realized.

Nelly groaned in frustration. Cy bent down to help her with the shoelace. "Thank you," Nelly murmured.

A minute into their conversation, Benno pointed out Nelly to the elderly woman, who peered at her, then shook her head. They signed some more, and the woman pointed to her companion. Benno thanked her and called, "Nelly!"

Nelly was walking in place, testing the tightness of the laces, and didn't answer. Cy nudged her. "That's you."

"Oh, right." Turning red, she hastened to where Benno was waving them over.

"Althea doesn't recognize you," he said, "and she knows practically every face in this town. Everyone says she's better than the phone book."

"So I'm probably not a local," Nelly said sullenly.

"Maybe. We're gonna try Delphine now."

They approached the woman by the van just as she pushed an apple basket all the way to the back and turned around. She cried out, "Benno!" and hugged him. "Oh, I haven't seen you in so long! Are you still looking for that little girl? Is she still missing?"

"We'll find her," he assured her. "I'm here on a different case, actually. We were wondering if you could help us."

"Of course!"

Benno gestured toward Nelly. "Do you happen to know this young lady?"

Delphine gave Nelly a hard stare. Nelly wasn't sure what to do, so she gave a tight-lipped smile.

After a minute, Delphine shook her head. "No, I'm sorry. Have we met?"

Nelly shrugged. "Not sure."

Delphine frowned. "You're not sure?"

Feeling she now owed an explanation, Nelly plunged on, "I—have amnesia. I woke up in the forest a few hours ago. I can't remember who I am or how I got here." She added a half-chuckle, trying to force her cheeks to stop burning.

Suddenly Delphine gave a small gasp and stared at Nelly with wide eyes. "Oh my…" she breathed.

"You do recognize her!" cried Cy.

Delphine pointed at Nelly. "You're the Lammwych girl, aren't you?"

Nelly looked at her blankly. "Lammwych?"

"The girl who disappeared into the forest and was never seen again. It was said you'd come back one day—in spirit, if not in person." She looked Nelly up and down in wonder. "You haven't aged a day!"

Benno frowned. "Aged?"

Cy asked, "When did this girl disappear?"

"Forty-two years ago!"

"Okay," said Nelly tightly as she did an about-face. Cy followed her and squeezed Nelly's shoulder. They left Benno to placate the old woman as she gabbed on about the Lammwych girl's return.

* * *

"You *bastard!* It's your fault! *Why didn't you say something earlier??!*" Sandra Toombs spewed a flood of invective as Deputy Derrick bodily restrained her from assaulting her ex-husband. He wasn't quick enough in the first second, as attested by a cut over the man's eye.

As Derrick escorted her down the hall toward the other end of the station, Sheriff Dubowski shut the door to his office and handed the wounded man a pack of alcohol wipes. Greg Toombs cleaned his cut, muttering curses under his breath. "So, while we're on the subject, Greg," the sheriff said sternly, "why *didn't* you say something sooner?"

"Because I honestly didn't think it was anything important!" Greg shouted. It was hard for him to tend to his wound and speak at the same time. "I don't always pick Megan up from school. It depends on, it...it's random!"

"But you were going to today."

"Yes."

"And before you could leave, you received this phone call."

"Yes."

"A call in which a man—whom you took to be an operator—asked for you by name, then apparently attempted to connect you with someone trying to get hold of you."

"I do business with computer companies in Japan. I thought it was one of their people trying to get in touch."

"And this phone call delayed you just enough that you weren't able to get to the school in time to pick up Megan."

"That's right. I got there and she'd already left, so I drove back home, thinking I'd get there at the same time she would."

"And it didn't occur to you until after we'd spent hours searching Wenskee Woods that that call might have been a deliberate ruse to prevent you from picking up your daughter, resulting in her taking the shortcut through the woods, where an abduction might be easier."

"I…I was just so worried about her. I wasn't thinking straight."

"So you thought of it later because you were less worried?"

"What—no! Look, what does it matter *when* I thought of it?! If someone kidnapped my daughter, it's not *my* fault. I'm not the one with enemies. You should be investigating Pressler!"

"Don't worry, we are. We know he's been involved in shady business deals around the country since long before he settled in Veil. We're also aware of the relationship between Elijah Pressler and your ex-wife."

"Oh, really?" Greg's lip curled in a humorless, unpleasant smile. "What all did she tell you?"

"I'm the one asking questions, Greg. If you think you have something to add to what we've learned, I'm all ears."

Greg threw aside the wipes. "How about this—she's not giving Pressler everything he wants. She pretends they're this happy couple—mostly to get back at me—but really they're having problems."

"Such as?"

"She's not giving him any money for his mayoral campaign."

"Pressler addressed that in public recently. He said he'd refused any donations from her in order to avoid nepotism."

"Bull. She's not spending money on him because she spends it all on Megan." His vehemence subsided for a moment. "It's the only thing I can't fault her for. But Pressler doesn't like coming second. He wants the attention on himself first."

"So he kidnapped his girlfriend's daughter to get money out of her...for his campaign?"

"Exactly!"

"But there hasn't been a ransom demand."

"Well...then maybe it's the other guy! The one he's running against for mayor!"

"Kurt Riner?"

"Yes! Maybe he kidnapped Megan to...to distract him! To take his attention away from his campaign!"

The sheriff eyed him dubiously. "If that's the case, then it's backfired. Pressler's using this crisis as a beacon to rally people behind him. They're gathering in the square as we speak."

Greg stood up. "I know you support Riner in the election! I know the two of you are friends! Are you not even going to investigate him?!"

Dubowski didn't rise to the bait. "Sit down, Greg. And relax. My senior deputy is at Riner's office right now, interviewing him and his staff."

* * *

Amy came into Kurt's outer office, where Deputy Grogan stood waiting. She chuckled lightly, as if amused. "Magenta Grogan," she said. "I heard you'd moved back to Veil."

"It's Jen," the deputy replied tightly. "Not Magenta."

"It's been a long time—Magenta. Did you miss all your old friends?"

Jen looked slightly nauseated. "I'm here to speak to your boss."

"Of course. He's expecting you." She made an after-you gesture toward the door, then went in first.

Jen entered to see Kurt Riner shaking hands with a smiling woman she recognized as a reporter from the local paper. "Thanks, Kelly," Riner said as the woman left. Jen noticed the woman exchange smiles with Amy as she exited. Then Riner turned to Jen. "Deputy, what can I do for you?"

Jen had met Riner once before, at a campaign fundraiser. Sheriff Dubowski had made an appearance and a speech to show his support; she had tagged along as his token deputy. She'd found Riner friendly and one of the most skilled small-talkers she'd ever met. She'd even found herself just beginning to like him—until she'd learned who the candidate's fiancée was. "I need to ask you some questions about the missing girl, Megan Toombs," she said, taking out her phone to make a recording of the interview.

"Yes, of course."

"I'm afraid some of these questions might be awkward."

"I understand." Riner sat on the edge of his desk and gestured for Jen to sit in a chair facing him, which she declined.

After stating the date and time, where she was, and whom she was with, she asked, "Have you ever met Megan Toombs?"

"I have not, but I know who she is."

"Can you clarify that?"

"I know she's the daughter of the woman my opponent, Elijah Pressler, is seeing romantically."

"Have you ever met Mrs. Toombs?"

"No. I saw her at the bank once, but we didn't speak."

"Do you have any idea at all where the girl might be?"

"I don't. I wish I did."

"Can you account for your whereabouts between eleven this morning and—"

Amy cut in, "Mr. Riner is under no obligation to answer any—"

"*Amy.*" Kurt Riner's voice was sharp, almost a bark, and Jen was startled at how quickly his face could suddenly take on a foreboding expression. A half-second later, when he turned back to her, he had reverted to his friendly facade, the ease of which made her trust him a great deal less. "Yes, I can," he said. "From ten-thirty to eleven-thirty, I was in a Skype meeting with a potential donor, and then I went to lunch with my fiancée"—he nodded toward Amy—"at Willow Grove. We got back to the office a little before one, and we've been here since."

"Can anyone corroborate that?"

"Yes, my staff can vouch for me, and they probably remember me at the restaurant. There was also a package delivered just before I left for lunch; I had to sign for it."

"Can you tell me whom you were Skyping with?"

"Yes, it was, uh—hold on, I'll get you his contact information."

"If you could also show me the delivery slip for the package— if they gave you one?"

"Yes, I think so. It's probably still out front." He left the office.

Amy watched carefully as Jen turned off the recording and put her phone away. Then she said scathingly, "Your boss could've at least given us a heads-up that we were going to be interrogated."

Jen gave her a strange look. "N-no, he really couldn't. For

one thing, it'd be unethical. For another, if someone found out, it would destroy the sheriff's integrity. Since Dubowski supports Riner in the election, your fiancé would lose voters."

Amy opened her mouth to protest—signifying that she considered the sheriff's support to be of very little value—but then hesitated and instead asked, "And what about you? Are you going to vote for us?"

"Us?" Jen repeated. "I didn't know you were running as co-candidates."

Amy didn't look amused. She glanced at the door to the outer office, and then said, without any trace of sympathy, "So I hear you're a widow now."

Jen's breath caught. Any hope she'd harbored of Amy having developed any sort of decency or kindness in the years since she'd left Veil was dashed. In as steady a voice as she could manage, she said, "More or less. He and I had split up."

"Must be hard on your kid."

"I have two of them."

"I thought they had different fathers."

"Yes, but—"

"How did this one die again?"

Jen could feel the heat rising in her cheeks, knew that her getting angry was exactly what Amy wanted—the same as when they were in school. Her father had always told her to match Amy's cruelty with calmness and maturity, but doing so had always felt like accepting the mistreatment. *How can she still be this way?!* Pulling out her phone again, she asked, "Why don't we talk about *your* whereabouts during the time that—"

"No, we've been over that. I was with Kurt all day today; he told you. I heard it was a fire that killed him," she went on without missing a beat.

"Amy—"

"Which seems pretty unlikely, to be honest."

Jen's thumb, which had been hovering over the button on her phone that would activate the recording mechanism, jerked away so fast she almost lost her grip. In a carefully controlled voice, she said, "What do you mean by that?"

"I just thought, being married to you, it's more likely he committed suicide."

They stared at each other, both of them waiting to see what Jen would do next. Jen could feel the reaction building up inside her, threatening to burst out, no matter how inappropriate it might be. In the end, she decided to just let it take its course and reap whatever repercussions might come.

She burst into laughter.

Amy was completely taken aback. It wasn't forced, contrived, or defiant laughter, just genuine, honest mirth.

"What's so funny?!" Amy demanded furiously.

Jen managed to calm down enough to say, "Are you serious? We're *adults,* Amy. I don't know about you, but having more than two decades between now and high school gives me a whole lot of perspective. If you really want to hurt me, if you *really* have nothing better to do, then you're going to have to up your game. Or, I don't know, you could act like a real adult and stop trying to be a bully."

"There's a difference between a bully and a winner," said Amy. "Maybe the reason you want to think you've changed is that you know you're still a loser. Losers like to be dramatic and talk about how life has put them through hell, how it's made them thick-skinned. So thick that when people like me take them down a peg, it's *nothing* to them, nothing in comparison to what they've suffered! Words can't hurt them anymore! But it's all just an act. They want to pretend they're better now, tougher, that they're not crying inside. If they really don't care what I tell them, if I really don't matter, why bother saying anything to me?" She gave Jen a knowing smirk.

Jen peered at Amy for several moments without speaking.

"Can't think of a response to that?" Amy gloated.

Jen drew a soft breath of realization, and when she spoke, it was mostly to herself. "This is about me being a deputy now. When I left Veil, I was your plaything, but now I'm a figure of authority, and you feel threatened."

"Oh, you wish!"

Jen didn't seem to have heard her. "Huh," she grunted. "Wonder why I didn't see that coming."

"You are so fake!" Amy spat, along with a few other things, but Jen, hearing Kurt's returning footsteps, had turned and was heading out to meet him.

V

"Let me be clear—this is not to say I'm not confident in Veil's law enforcement agency! But Megan's been missing for four hours now, and the sheriff's department hasn't been able to find her—not to mention they keep changing their minds as to where they should search. That tells me this is a job so big it needs more people to get it done— more than just the four or five deputies the sheriff has at his disposal."

Nelly, Cy, and Deputy Benno had had no luck at the farmers' market. Their next idea was to mingle with the massing crowd in the square. With so many people there, if anyone in town knew Nelly (even if she was only visiting), there was a chance they might see her and address her. The trio alighted from the patrol car at the edge of the square, just in time for Nelly to hear the booming voice. "This is a job for the *whole* community," the voice went on, "and I'm happy to see so many of you here, ready to do your part to help your neighbor!" As applause followed his speech, Nelly spotted the speaker standing atop a small platform, holding a megaphone. Her first impression of him was that she recognized him, giving her a brief flash of hope, only to be disappointed a moment later when she realized she'd never seen him before (as far as she knew). Everything about his appearance—the sharp angles of his handsome face, the curly hair just a shade too dark to be believable, the brightness of his teeth, the jacket that was slightly too thin for this chilly weather—suggested this was a celebrity, or at least someone whose identity she was *supposed* to know, even though she didn't.

She and Cy glanced at Benno, who nodded at the speaker. "Pressler," he said.

"My assistant, Ernie, and I are going to break you into groups of eight. We've worked out a search grid covering—"

"Excuse me!" called a male voice. "I have a question!"

Cy's eyes widened. *"Oh no."*

Nelly craned her neck along with the rest of the crowd to see who had spoken. She recognized that voice.

"I'll answer questions in just a minute," said Pressler. "First let's get the search organized."

"I'm just confused on something," the shouter continued, stepping forward where more people could see him. It was Rob. He pointed off to the right. "Are those guys with the cameras part of the search party, too?"

Dozens of heads turned, though Pressler's didn't. His eyes remained on Rob as he pressed his lips together in annoyance.

Deputy Benno chuckled softly and shook his head, regarding the cameramen on the roof of a building across the street. They probably would've gone unnoticed if no one had pointed them out. A murmuring spread through the crowd.

"Your online rallying cry said this effort was non-political," Rob went on, stepping closer to Pressler. "So why would you need cameras?"

"We can—" Pressler interrupted himself and handed off the megaphone to his assistant. Raising his voice, he responded,

"We can address this after we find Megan. Right now, that's all that matters. If you delay us, you're forcing her to wait longer to be rescued."

"Rescued? Are you saying she's being held hostage?"

The murmur in the crowd grew to a chatter.

"Of course not!" Pressler looked left and right and made placating gestures to the crowd. "To my knowledge, no one knows what's happened to her, but wherever she is, she's not home with her mother, where she belongs! *That's* the situation she needs to be rescued from."

"And where is her mother? Why isn't she here?"

"I'm not aware of her current whereabouts, but that's not—"

"She's at the sheriff's station, as I think you know. Is there a reason you don't want to mention the sheriff? Or at least that you don't want to mention him in a way that shows he's still working on the case? Maybe because the sheriff is publicly opposed to you and your campaign?"

As the argument continued, Cy turned away and said in a low, unsteady voice, "I can't do this. I can't stay here and watch him pretend to be the hero. I don't want to run away from him, but if I stay, I'm going to do something I…"

Nelly leaned in and whispered, "No—do it."

Cy blinked and gave her a startled look. "What?"

"Whatever your gut's telling you to do, do it now."

At first Cy balked, even started to shake her head, but then she looked back at her ex-boyfriend, heckling—harassing—his latest victim. Her jaw set in determination.

"It seems to me," jeered Rob, gesturing carelessly at the camera crew across the street, "you're more worried about upping your chances at being elected than finding your girlfriend's missing daughter."

Pressler had for the most part managed to keep his cool thus far, but now he pointed at the cameras with growing impatience. "That is not important right now!"

"Are you saying those cameras aren't yours?"

"If any media wants to cover these events—"

"Those aren't media! *I'm* with the media, and those aren't ours."

"Rob Mulroy!"

Many people flinched and covered their ears, startled by the voice from the megaphone. Pressler spun around to see Cy holding it, standing on the platform, his bemused assistant standing nearby.

The teenage girl boomed, "If you're not going to help with the search, you shouldn't be here, Rob. And you're not 'with the media,' you're an intern!"

Rob stared at her, flustered. She stared right back at him, no longer timid but confident, imperious.

Scattered whispers—"Who's that? Why does she have the megaphone?"—shot through the crowd, but with the intensity of the look she directed at Rob, it could have been just the two of them there and no one else.

Rob barked a short, condescending laugh. "I have every right to be here," he said. "And you had your chance to talk to me. I didn't think you were this petty—"

"I said you can leave!" Cy's voice thundered.

"And what if I don't?"

"Then I have two words for you. Don't make me use them."

"What two words?!"

Cy smiled slightly. "Skin allergy."

All of Rob's swagger vanished. His shoulders tensed, his lips parted, and his eyes stopped blinking.

Pressler, watching him, raised a curious eyebrow.

"Do you want me to say more?" asked Cy.

Nelly looked on her friend with pride.

Indecision and anger played across Rob's face. He seemed torn between two actions: making off in haste or marching up to Cy to confront her. In the end, he took one faltering step toward her—only to find Deputy Benno suddenly between him and his ex. The deputy folded his arms and leveled a falsely bland stare at him, as if to say, *Go on, try it.*

Rob decided not to. After a moment he raised his hands, acknowledging defeat, and strode off without looking back.

Pressler, suppressing laughter, turned to Cy with a broad smile and began applauding, widening his arms to their full extent between each clap. The onlookers soon followed his example, and within moments Cy found herself the object of thunderous applause. She wasn't sure what to do. She glanced at Nelly, who grinned at her and gave her a thumbs-up. Cy looked back at the crowd, muttered, "Oh, what the hell," and took a grand bow.

As Pressler approached her, she started to hold out the megaphone to him, but then hesitated. "Actually, could I keep this for a second?"

Pressler made a sweeping, magnanimous gesture. "The floor is yours!"

Deputy Benno rolled his eyes.

Stepping back onto the platform, Cy waved. "Hi, everyone. My name is Cyanne Grogan. My mom's one of the sheriff's deputies. Um…" She glanced again at Nelly, who drew a deep breath, realizing what she was about to do. Cy said, "I need to ask if anyone knows this woman. She was injured and she doesn't know who she is. She has amnesia. It's possible what happened to her is connected to Megan's disappearance, so if anyone can tell us who she is, it might help us find Megan. Anyone?"

Many people lurched forward, all trying at once to get a look at Nelly's face. Nelly tensed, feeling a sense of bombardment. Cy stepped down, gently took her hand, and led her to the platform, where Nelly gave another half-hearted wave.

Having a hundred people staring at you, examining you, made you dizzy, Nelly found. She took deep breaths and directed her gaze over the people, to the mountains in the distance towering over the tree line.

"I think I've seen her," said a hesitant voice nearby. Cy and Nelly turned to see Pressler's assistant, the small, thirtyish man with glasses and neat brown hair, giving his head a bowl-top appearance.

"You know her, Ernie?" Pressler asked as he approached.

"No, I don't know her, but I'm pretty sure I saw her, or someone with her hairstyle."

Nelly put a hand to her hair, evidently wondering what style she had.

"Where did you see her?" asked Cy.

"At Hockney's, this morning when I was picking up a tape measure. I'm pretty sure she was in the paint aisle."

"The hardware store?"

"That's right."

Cy started to head to the patrol car with Nelly and Benno, then realized she still had the megaphone. Embarrassed, she returned it to Pressler, who held out his hand for her to shake. "I'm much obliged to you, Miss Grogan," he said as they shook.

"Sure, no problem," she replied, blushing, then went on her way.

"All right, everyone, we have our own mystery to solve. Ernie?" He nodded to his assistant, who began handing printouts of maps to the crowd. Pressler set down the megaphone and picked up another set of maps to hand out—and then did a double take. Two people were crossing the park, heading straight toward him.

Just as Nelly was about to get back in the patrol car, she, too, saw the two new arrivals, and noticed that the crowd's chatter had died down, all eyes on the newcomers.

"That's Kurt Riner, the attorney," said Deputy Benno upon seeing Nelly's look of curiosity. "He's running against Pressler for mayor. And that's Amy Chester, his fiancée. She's acting as his campaign manager. I wondered if they'd show up."

Kurt Riner looked slightly younger than Pressler, though taller, beefier, with close-cropped hair and a thick goatee. Amy Chester looked extremely thin next to him, with blond hair that was dark at the roots, and dark eyebrows. Both of them were smiling, but only Riner's smile looked genuine.

"Kurt, Amy," Pressler greeted them lightly as if he wasn't at all surprised to see them. "I'm glad you made it."

"Well, Megan can use all the help she can get," answered Kurt.

Throughout the crowd, a multitude of camera-phones were lifted and pictures snapped.

Pressler handed Kurt and Amy a map. "You can join the group that's going to search out by the old fire station, on County Road Four."

"Sounds good," said Kurt. Then he lowered his voice slightly and added, "And just for the record, this doesn't mean I don't have confidence in the sheriff's department."

"Of course." Pressler beamed at him.

"Wait," said Amy in growing alarm. "County Road Four—

that's near the landfill." She wrinkled her nose.

Pressler's face took on a look of bemused astonishment. "Oh, well, if you'd like to switch to a different area—"

"Nope." Riner clapped a hand on Amy's shoulder and squeezed. "Nothing like that. She was just clarifying the location."

Pressler beamed again and repeated, "Of course."

Every eye in the crowd was on the two mayoral candidates, waiting to see if their front of good-natured camaraderie would fade away to reveal something more cutthroat. Every eye... except those of one person: a rake-thin, middle-aged man with unkempt, graying hair who had been slowly, steadily backing away through the crowd for some time now. His eyes were fixed not on the competitors, but on the young woman who couldn't remember her name, now being driven away in a patrol car. Once she was no longer within his sight, he sidled away and crossed the street, his eyes downcast, as if hoping that by not looking at anyone, he'd be less noticeable.

But someone did notice him. One person had caught sight of him staring—with recognition—at Nelly.

Rob Mulroy set out to follow the nervous man with gray hair.

VI

"I don't think she's remembering anything," Cy whispered to Deputy Benno. They'd been at the hardware store for fifteen minutes, most of which Nelly had spent in the paint aisle, scanning cans and brushes shelf by shelf. Lately she'd been shifting from foot to foot restlessly, clearly having lost interest.

"Give her time," Benno advised her. Then he glanced over and with a grunt of interest said, "Birdbaths," and headed in that direction.

Nelly emerged from the paint aisle with a wry expression. "They have a color called 'blue planet blue.' I think I'd remember that if I'd been here."

"Nothing seems familiar to you?"

Nelly shook her head. "It doesn't make sense anyway. In a town this small, someone would've recognized me by now, even if I was just visiting. I must be a passer-through—in which case, why would I be buying paint?"

"I don't know," Cy shrugged. "That guy, Ernie, was awfully sure it was you he saw here. Maybe you weren't looking for paint but just happened to be in that aisle when he noticed you."

Nelly sighed, glancing around the store to see if anything sparked her interest.

Cy glanced downward. "Thanks, by the way, for what you said in the park, for pushing me to...you know."

Nelly smiled. "How did it feel?"

Cy couldn't help but smile back. "It felt great. I...I felt like myself again." Her smile faltered. "I've kind of been shutting everybody out since...since Dad died. I guess I didn't realize I was making myself miserable."

"I'm sorry." Hesitating, Nelly touched Cy's upper arm lightly. "When did he pass away?"

"In June. Mom and I moved here just after. She said it would help. Give us a fresh start. I think it did the opposite." Resentment tinged her words.

"Maybe she thought coming back to her roots would help build a support for you both," Nelly suggested.

Cy shook her head, her eyes narrowing. "She didn't need support. She and Dad separated earlier this year. I barely got to see him the last few months; I was stuck with her." Cy paused. "She's not that sorry he's gone." Resentment was clearly shifting to anger. As Deputy Benno approached, she blinked emotion away and said, more loudly, "Well, if you're a passer-through, then you must've come either by car or by bus. If you have a car, then it'll probably be found abandoned soon. We could take you to the bus station and see if anyone who works there recognizes... Um, Nelly?"

Nelly was staring past Cy, transfixed. She stepped around the girl, reached up, and touched a price tag for a cordless drill combo kit.

Cy exchanged excited glances with Benno. "You remember something?"

"I'm...not sure."

"Something about the drill kit?" asked Benno.

"No." Her eyes weren't on the drill kit at all, just the price tag, denoting the cost of the item as $127.95. "One, two, seven." She squinted, mentally straining. "Those numbers…"

Cy straightened in realization. To Benno she said, "I know where we need to go next."

Five minutes later saw them back in the patrol car, passing a sign informing them they were crossing the village limits. Nelly was fascinated by Veil's layout. It was decidedly a small town, but because it was built on a slope, it was hard to see all at once. Twice she'd had the impression they were leaving town, only to discover they'd curved and ascended to a higher section with more houses, some of whose front rooms had been converted to local specialty stores. One sold baseball cards; another, ice skates.

"Before Veil was built, there was a highway that people used to travel between the bigger towns nearby," Benno explained. "When our town came along, they built a new highway that intersected us, and the old one became a back road. Barely anybody uses it now—probably why it's not on that map. This is the only way to get to it by car." He turned onto a dirt road that veered sharply and steeply downward.

Nelly leaned forward. At the bottom of the slope, beside a stop sign, was a rusty, faded green sign denoting the crossroad as County Road 127.

Benno stopped at the T-intersection. "Left or right?"

Cy glanced at Nelly, but the woman seemed in a kind of wide-eyed trance. "Left," Cy told Benno. Benno complied. The car turned and drove slowly along a level, dusty road, tall grass and fire-colored trees on either side.

Cy's anger from earlier had not quite abated. She turned her gaze away from the vibrant foliage to take deep breaths, all the while scowling at the back of the seat in front of her. Deputy Benno must have seen her expression. "Not a fan of autumn?" he asked.

She glared at him in the rearview mirror. "It's very pretty," she grumbled. "It doesn't mean I have to like living here."

"Living here or moving here?"

"What's the difference?"

A silver SUV passed them, driving the other way. "Well," said Benno, "you and your mom *moved* here because your dad passed away, so that's got a permanently bad association for you. But *living* here…"

Cy exhaled slowly, starting to relax. "I hadn't thought of it like that."

"You can be angry and still enjoy your life here," Benno went on, almost to himself. "You don't have to blame Veil for what happened."

Cy all but growled, "I don't blame the town, I blame…"

She hesitated, and just then Nelly lurched forward in her seat, staring out the side window. "Stop here!" she cried. Benno pulled over and opened the doors so the women could get out. Nelly immediately shot across the road—and it was a good thing that the road was scarcely used, for she barely checked for oncoming traffic. She dropped to her knees and brushed her fingers against a large rock sitting in the tall grass. "I was here," she breathed.

"This morning?" asked Cy.

"I—don't know," said Nelly. "But I remember being here. I remember this place. I remember…" She closed her eyes and didn't speak for several seconds.

Benno came over and examined the rock, particularly an area on top that was stained brown. "Blood," he whispered to Cy.

Her eyes still shut, Nelly winced and sucked in air through her teeth.

"Nelly?" Cy approached her, concerned.

"Something hit me," Nelly whispered. "Hit me—everywhere. At once. Then there was…something tickling my nose. Grass. I was lying with my face in it. I tried to push myself up, but my arms wouldn't move. I lifted my head, and there was blood on the ground right in front of my eyes, blood from my head. I think I…I passed out again. But then I remember…crawling… crawling alongside the road. I was trying to…trying to…"

"To find help?"

"No…no, I wasn't looking for help… Why wasn't I?" She shook her head, flummoxed. "Why wouldn't I have been looking for help? What was I looking for?"

Benno leaned in toward Cy and said in a low voice, "Maybe she wasn't looking for anything. Maybe she was trying to get away from something. Or someone."

"From whom?" Cy whispered back.

Nelly had trailed off, her head tilted, gazing off into the distance. She frowned. "A car," she said.

Cy blinked. "You remember a car?"

"No, I mean there's a car coming down the road." She pointed.

Cy and Benno turned to see an SUV approaching. It would pass them in a few seconds.

Nelly drew back in slowly growing alarm. "That's the same car as earlier."

"What do you mean?"

"It's the one that went by us a few minutes ago, going the other way."

"I doubt that," said Benno.

The silver SUV slowed and pulled over behind the patrol car.

The three of them glanced at each other.

Several seconds passed, and the SUV did nothing, merely sat there, idling, on the side of the road.

Cy and Nelly drew close behind the deputy, who flashed his badge and called, "I'm Deputy Benno of the Veil sheriff's department. Can you tell me your name, please?"

Whoever was in the SUV didn't respond. The sun was getting low in the sky, brightening it in just the right spot such that the light was reflected off the windows, preventing the three of them from seeing the driver.

Leaning sideways, Nelly observed that the front of the vehicle bore no license plate. She couldn't see the back of it.

Benno took a couple steps forward. "I said, I'm from the Veil sheriff's department. Please identify yourself!"

Still no reply. All of a sudden the wheels began rotating backward, turning slightly, bringing the SUV back onto the road, reversing it farther and farther.

"Get back in the car," Benno ordered. They crossed the road, keeping an eye on the SUV, now a hundred meters away. It swerved, beginning to turn around.

Benno got into the patrol car first and began speaking on the radio as he started the engine. Cy got in without any trouble, but Nelly's overlarge boot got caught in the door and nearly came off her foot. She struggled to tug the boot back on before closing the door.

Thus the door was still open when the SUV smashed into them from behind.

Benno's head struck the steering wheel and he was immediately knocked out. Cy had half-turned automatically to see what had hit them, and so was bodily slammed along her right side into the seat in front of her. She shrieked in pain and terror and tried to open her door, but of course there was no way to open it from the inside. Nelly seized her arm and tugged her in the other direction.

The car was still moving but slowing as Nelly and Cy stumbled from the wrecked vehicle. The SUV had braked several meters back, its front dented from the impact.

Cy banged on the front window. "Benno!"

The SUV's driver door opened. Then another door. And another.

Nelly grabbed Cy and shouted, "Come on!" and led her at a sprint across the road, through the tall grass. They glanced back and glimpsed three figures moving toward the patrol car, but they never stopped running, even when they plunged into the trees.

VII

Elijah Pressler made a show of waving away the ever-present cameras as Sandra Toombs rushed, sobbing, into his arms, and when one camera still flashed, he glared overtly at the person holding it.

Sheriff Dubowski shook his head from where he stood by his patrol car, which he had just used to transport Sandra here, to join Pressler's search group by the footbridge over Greene River. The sheriff was quite sure, despite the play-acting, that Pressler fully intended for at least one photo of him comforting the anxious mother to make it to the public eye. Indeed, the camera operators had long since given up trying to remain inconspicuous.

The sheriff had protested against Sandra leaving the station, telling her he needed to know immediately if she was contacted with a ransom demand. She'd argued that such a demand was equally likely to be made of Pressler, with the purpose of forcing him to step down from the election. Secretly Dubowski suspected that if there really was going to be a ransom demand, it would've been made by now, but it was clear that Sandra was nearing hysterics and needed reassurance that could only come from one person, so he gave in. (Besides, this gave him an excuse to keep an eye on Pressler.)

"Thanks for bringing her, Sheriff," Pressler said to him solemnly, as if personal transportation had been the most useful action Dubowski had performed today. It rankled the sheriff that it felt true.

"You can't just let him act like we're his taxi service!" Apparently it rankled Deputy Derrick, too.

"Keep your voice down, Deputy," the sheriff replied as they traipsed along behind the search party, led by the mayoral candidate and his girlfriend.

It seemed to cost the deputy an effort to limit his voice to an outraged whisper. "He keeps trying to boss us around—he's acting like he's mayor already!"

"Real mayors don't act that way toward law enforcement, but I know what you mean."

"He keeps saying he wishes the sheriff's department had found Megan by now. He's trying to remind everyone, convince them we're incompetent. He's making them think we're morons. I bet, if he could get away with it, he'd even accuse us of trying to run him out of the election by kidnapping Megan ourselves!"

The sheriff felt his patience waning. Privately he agreed with his deputy about Pressler's ulterior motives, but he tired of the diatribe. "The only thing people are thinking about right now is that hopefully the kid'll be found and brought back safe and sound," he said.

Still somehow managing to keep his furious gaze directed at Pressler without tripping on the uneven ground, Derrick went on, "He made a joke earlier about us not being able to make up our minds where to search, how we kept switching between Wenskee Woods and Mountain Boulevard. If Grogan had just kept her mouth shut, he wouldn't have been able to—"

The two men almost collided as Sheriff Dubowski suddenly stepped in front of his deputy and halted, turning to face him at the same time. The deputy had a good four inches on him, but the steely look in the sheriff's eyes made the younger man's knees quiver. "We made a mistake," the sheriff hissed, and then amended, "*I* made a mistake. And *Senior Deputy* Grogan caught it before it went too far. She did her job. If all you're really worried about is our public image, think how much more we would've looked like idiots if she hadn't been there."

Derrick's facial muscles twitched. He managed to look his superior in the eye and respond, reservedly, "Yes, sir."

The sheriff started to speak again, but paused as a man trotted past them, heading for the search party, trying to catch up. Once the man was out of earshot, the sheriff said, more levelly, "Jimmy, I know what happened with the promotion wasn't what you were expecting. I know you're probably still angry with me, but—"

"No, sir! I'm not angry at you. Not at all." Derrick's eyes were wide with sincerity. "I wasn't trying to do a good job just for the promotion. You can count on me, sir. Always. I promise."

"Then you're going to have to find a way to accept the way things are. If we aren't all able to work as a team, we're liable to *keep* looking like idiots, again and again."

"*Pressler!*"

Derrick and Dubowski turned to see the search party several meters ahead, and in between, Greg Toombs—the man who had passed them a moment ago.

"Like now," muttered the sheriff.

As Greg neared the group of searchers, Pressler's assistant, Ernie, stepped gallantly in front of Sandra. "Mr. Toombs, you keep away from her!"

The woman pushed Ernie roughly aside so she could face down her ex-husband, herself. "I don't want you near me," she spat.

"Then leave," he returned evenly. "I have something to ask your boyfriend."

"And what's that?" said Pressler.

Greg took a step closer to him, fury smoldering in his eyes. "Where is my daughter?" he growled.

Pressler shot a look of commiseration at his girlfriend before replying, "That's what we're all trying to find out—"

"No, you know!" Greg shouted, taking another step forward. "You know where she is! Just looking at you, I can tell! If it was about ransom, then there would've been a message from the kidnapper by now. No, this is about getting attention, and you love getting attention the most out of anyone in this town! Now, what have you done with her?!"

Pressler gave the man a long, stony glare. He was perhaps an inch shorter, but the attitude he carried was that of a man looking at something far beneath him. "You know what?" he said, affecting false mildness. "I think you're right. I think this motive *is* personal." And to the sheriff's great discomfiture, Pressler stepped brazenly forward, just to within arm's reach of his accuser. "What could be more personal than a man losing his wife and seeing her choose someone new, someone more successful, more *desirable* than he could ever be?"

"Gentlemen," the sheriff rumbled warningly.

"So," Pressler went on tauntingly, "to drive his rival away, this man stages the kidnapping of *his own daughter*. Never mind what kind of hell it puts the mother through," he said, gesturing at his girlfriend. "All he can think about is setting up the object of his envy."

The sheriff cast a quick glance at Sandra, curious about her reaction to this theory. She looked skeptical but uncertain.

"So what's the next step?" Pressler continued. "How does this plan culminate? I own several properties throughout Veil. Do you have Megan stashed in one of them? Maybe there won't be a ransom demand, but there might be a tip—an anonymous tip—to the sheriff's department, telling them to check one of those properties, and there they find her, bound and gagged but otherwise unharmed, never knowing the person who selfishly scarred her for life was her own f—"

Everyone knew the attack was coming, the way Pressler was egging the man on. The cameras had been fixed on the two of them like vultures. Most likely, Pressler was expecting a right hook and intended to duck, but Greg Toombs either anticipated this or simply believed in expediency.

His foot snapped out, catching Pressler neatly in the groin.

For a few minutes all was chaos—cameras clicking, onlookers cringing, Sandra yelling, Pressler writhing on the ground, the sheriff and his deputy restraining a violently thrashing Greg. By the time Pressler was able to sit up without wincing, he found himself alone with Dubowski. "I sent the others on ahead," the sheriff told him. "If you're feeling up to it, I can escort you to them."

"Thank you, Sheriff, but I don't need an escort. Remember, before I moved to the city and started my career, I grew up in Veil. I know these woods even better than you, a *former forest ranger*." He gave Dubowski a look the sheriff didn't understand.

Setting his puzzlement aside, the sheriff said, "We're charging Greg Toombs."

"Good," Pressler croaked, starting to stand. Dubowski offered him a hand, but Pressler waved it away. On his feet, he said to the sheriff, "What he accused me of—kidnapping Megan for 'attention'—did you believe him?"

"Not without evidence."

Pressler scoffed. "That's fine for you. But voters don't need evidence to believe the worst. Sheriff, I authorize you to search all the properties in Veil that I own. My secretary can provide you with a complete list."

Dubowski licked his lips. "That won't be necessary, thank you."

Pressler narrowed his eyes. "What do you mean, that won't be necessary?"

"I sent my deputies to investigate your properties"—he glanced at his watch—"ninety minutes ago. Technically, without a warrant, none of them could go inside—not without probable cause—but now that we have your go-ahead, that's all academic." The sheriff gave Pressler a pleasant smile and waited to see what he did next.

After several moments of staring, Pressler returned the smile. "On the record, Sheriff, I'm glad our town has so capable a leader in a crisis such as this."

"And off the record?"

"Off the record…Mr. Toombs is frantic over his daughter, so I won't take his assault personally."

Dubowski frowned. "I don't see the connection."

"When I *do* take something personally…there are consequences."

* * *

Nelly was remembering.

She could remember it all so vividly—how she woke up on the gravel just off the shoulder of the highway, how it was too painful to move, how frightened she felt, how she finally rolled herself over onto her back by twisting her legs, how she sat up and touched her forehead where it was wet, how her fingers came away wet and sticky…

There was something missing.

Missing how? Missing from her memory? No, it wasn't that. When she woke up by the road, some *thing* was missing. Something should've been there that wasn't. *Something should have been there.*

Was that what frightened her? Was that why she'd fled into the woods, wandering aimlessly until she came across Cyanne, who waved her hand before her eyes and said, "Nelly!" over and over again?

Wait. That wasn't what had happened then. That was happening *now*.

"Nelly! Are you okay?"

"Cy? Wh-what happened?"

Relieved, Cy answered, "You went blank on me for a minute. Like a seizure or something. Is your head hurting?"

Nelly brushed her fingertips against the bandage over her forehead. "No. But it's happening again, I—I'm having trouble telling past from present."

Cy gestured for her to sit down. "Do you think those guys in the SUV are the ones who…who injured you and made you forget?"

Slowly Nelly shook her head. "I don't think so. It doesn't feel right." She peered through the trees behind her.

"I think we lost them," Cy told her. "I tried calling Mom, but there's no cell service out here. We need to get back to town before it gets dark. If we get stuck out here at night, we're screwed."

Nelly looked up at the sky, which had dimmed and turned

overcast, hiding the location of the sun. "Do you know how to get back?" she asked with growing anxiety.

"N-no, but...but Veil was built around a river, and rivers mean lower elevation, so if we head for lower ground..." She caught sight of Nelly's face growing paler. "Hey," she said, touching her arm gently. "We're gonna get back, okay? We'll be all right."

In a trembling voice Nelly asked, "How cold does it get at night?"

"We're not gonna get stuck out here. I'm sorry, I shouldn't have said—"

"I don't wanna die!"

"You won't! Nelly—!"

Nelly felt mortified at the way she was acting, but she had to say it. "I don't want to die...not knowing who I am."

Cy put her arms around her and held her. "You're not going to. I promise." She went on holding her, and after a minute Nelly drew a deep breath, ready to go on in the direction Cy had indicated.

Without the time limit imposed by the sun's descent toward the horizon, the journey through the woods might have been pleasant. Leaves whispered when stirred by a gentle breeze. Now and again the women glimpsed the twitching nose or flashing tail of a rabbit or chipmunk. Here and there they came across flowers, some of which Nelly (to her surprise) knew the names of.

They didn't speak much, saving their breath to keep the pace quick. Thus it seemed a non-sequitur to Nelly when Cy stopped in her tracks and said, "I'm an idiot." Before Nelly could ask for clarification, Cy began climbing the nearest tree.

It was a tall pine—or at least something coniferous that looked like a pine (apparently Nelly wasn't as well-versed in the classification of trees). Concerned over the waning daylight, Nelly called up from the base of the tree, asking what Cy was doing. Cy's reply was, "Augh! Dammit!" followed by her rapid downward climb. "I couldn't get high enough," she complained. "The top boughs aren't sturdy enough. They broke when I pulled on them."

Nelly said, realizing, "You were trying to get above the tree line, to see the town from up high."

"Yeah. It'd be nice if I could see which trees are highest from down here. We could keep trying, but we might lose all our time."

Nelly scanned the area, concentrating on the tree trunks. The larger the trunk, she reasoned, the older the tree, and therefore the higher—

She did a double take.

Cy noticed, and said, "What is it?"

"I think I saw something!" Nelly sped off, Cy scampering behind.

For several minutes they sprinted through the trees. Cy kept glancing downward to watch for roots and rocks waiting to trip her, but Nelly's gaze was fixated ahead, so much so that it was a wonder she never lost her footing.

"Nelly!" Cy finally called. "I don't see any…" She trailed off as a small building came into view, a rundown metal shack. *But we've come hundreds of feet,* Cy thought to herself. *There's no way Nelly could've seen it from all the way back there!*

A rusty, faded sign identified the shack as Ranger Station 5. From the dilapidated state it was in, they could tell it hadn't been in use for several years.

"I don't suppose there's a phone or a radio inside," Nelly wheezed, catching her breath.

"I wouldn't bet on it, but there might be a map or someth—" Cy broke off and gave Nelly a look of alarm. Nelly returned the look. She'd heard it, too.

As one, they lunged for the door of the shack and heaved it open. The muffled cries and squeals from within became louder. There were, of course, no working lights inside, but enough daylight shone dimly through the door to reveal a small, struggling form lying on its side. Nelly and Cy found the person's arms and helped them sit up. "Oh my god, Megan!" Cy exclaimed, tugging at the gag covering the girl's tear-stained face.

VIII

"Following the assault, Mr. Toombs was placed under arrest *and is currently incarcerated at the Veil Sheriff's Station. Elijah Pressler purports to be uninjured and continues to lead the volunteer search efforts throughout the rural areas surrounding the village.*"

The building that served as Veil's radio station was one of the oldest in the town. Many considered it a historical landmark. Relatively speaking, it wouldn't be too long before the station celebrated its centennial, and as such it would be unthinkable to move to a new facility. Any upgrades would have to be made onsite. One result of this was a surfeit of outdated equipment accumulated in various storage rooms as well as the basement. In one of these rooms, the equipment had been rearranged into a work area, with a halogen desk lamp, magnifying glass, and other tools.

As the anchor's voice blared throughout the building through a set of speakers, into this work area stumbled the man with gray hair.

For a moment, he swayed in the doorway. He hadn't run here—to do so would have drawn attention to himself that he didn't want—yet his breath came hard and fast, his legs quivering. He grabbed for the door handle, missed, and fell to his knees. He crawled across the room, tugged with his fingertips at an old switchboard leaning against the wall, and, straining, managed to pull it apart, revealing a makeshift hidden compartment. From inside he drew a sheaf of papers covered with scribbled handwriting, blotched here and there with old stains. Pivoting clumsily on the floor, the man stuffed the papers into a metal waste bin, crushing them down with his fist. Then, with shaking hands, he ignited a match and tossed it in, setting the papers ablaze. As smoke issued from the bin, he staggered to his feet, crossed the room and yanked on a chain descended from a small square high on the wall. The exterior lid opened and the exhaust fan activated, venting the smoke from the room.

His goal accomplished, the man sagged into a wooden chair with a raggedy cushion. He reached down, fumbled at yet another hiding place, and withdrew a bottle of whiskey.

The bottle was inches from his lips when he noticed he wasn't alone. Someone was standing in the doorway. It was a tall young man. His face was in shadow, but his glasses reflected the firelight from the bin.

The older man's heart was pounding, but he did his best to sound tough, baring his teeth, as if biting each syllable. "If you ain't got legitimate business here, sonny, then you're trespassing."

The younger man stepped into the room. He looked vaguely familiar. "I just came to see if it was ready yet."

"Huh?"

"You're Mr. Fleagle, aren't you? Tuck Fleagle?"

Tuck's heart fluttered in terror, but his voice remained steady. "You know my name."

"Y-yeah. We sort of met this morning."

Tuck blinked in confusion and surprise. He squinted at the young man.

"I'm sorry," said the stranger, "we were only in the same room for a second. I'm Rob Mulroy from the *Veil Chronicle*. This morning I dropped off a Q8 recording. You were gonna convert it to an MP3 file."

Relief flooded Tuck's insides, but he remained surly. "I haven't had a chance yet! In case you haven't heard, there's a little girl missing. I was helping with the search. Damn deputies don't know what they're doing."

"Oh, that's right!" exclaimed Mulroy. "You were at the square earlier, with the other volunteers. But then you left before the search actually got started." The young man's tone had changed, just slightly, into something less ingenuous.

Tuck felt a chill creep up his spine, as if he'd walked into some sort of trap.

"You left right after you saw that girl," Mulroy went on. "The one with amnesia—supposedly." He cast a deliberate glance down at the bin and its smoldering contents. "It almost looked as if you recognized her, or at least knew who she was."

Tuck Fleagle had been holding the bottle aloft all this time. Now, as he stood, he set it down heavily, the whiskey sloshing, spattering out over the desk. "I don't know nothin' about that girl," he said stolidly but unconvincingly.

As if reading the terror in Tuck's eyes, a broad smile stretched across Mulroy's face, his eyes gleaming greedily. "So it's that good, huh?"

Tuck gave him a strange look. "'Good'?"

"I mean, what is she, a criminal? Fugitive?" He took out a small notebook and golf pencil. "Or something bigger? Like royalty, or a movie star who's had plastic surgery?" When Tuck only stared at him, Mulroy began writing, speaking out loud as he did so. "Radio technician Tuck Fleagle identifies amnesiac as—"

Frantically Tuck shushed him, waving his arms in a frenzy.

"Listen, Tuck, I can make up whatever I want and report that you told it to me, so if you don't want to be misquoted, you might as well give me the truth."

Tuck's eyes rolled up and he uttered a long groan, shaking his head. The groan lasted so long that as he ran his hand through his thinning hair, it broke into raspy laughter. "Iiiiidiot," he slurred. He glared at Mulroy with a mix of contempt and pity. "You really think anyone would believe what I tell you? Maybe you haven't been in town too long."

"I've been here long enough."

"Then you should know I'm the town kook. The conspiracy theorist. The drunk crackpot. No one in Veil cares what I say."

"Then why are you afraid to talk?"

After a moment Tuck laughed again, but it sounded more forced. "'Cause I'm crazy," he said, shrugging. "The things I do don't make sense. Get used to it." He sat back down and took a swig from the bottle.

"Look, Mr. Fleagle," Mulroy said in an oily voice, "if you want, I can just make you an anonymous source. You can tell me whatever you want, and if the people read it without knowing it was you who said it…well, they might actually listen. Right?" He chuckled. "I mean, think about it. It'd be like you're tricking them into taking you seriously. Wouldn't that be nice, for once?"

Tuck's mouth stretched into a grin that matched Mulroy's. He leaned forward and whispered, "I don't care about being taken seriously, kid. I let go of that a long time ago."

Mulroy looked away a moment, biting his lip. "Well…what about the girl? Do you care about her?"

Tuck narrowed his eyes at him.

Mulroy went on, "I mean, she must be in hell, not knowing her own name, no clue who her family is or where she belongs." He gave an exaggerated shrug. "If only someone knew, and could tell her."

Tuck's smile had completely disappeared, replaced by a grim sneer. Mulroy laughed at him. "I might buy that you don't care about yourself anymore, Mr. Fleagle, but deep down, I think you still have a soft spot for others. Far as I can see, I'm the only one who can you help you…to help her."

Tuck muttered something too soft for Mulroy to hear, which was probably just as well. "Fine," Tuck barked. "I'll tell you. But not here."

"What do you mean, not here?"

"Meet me tonight, midnight, at the lot where they have the farmers' market."

"Come on, man, I'm not letting you disappear on me. Just tell me now."

"You moron, we're in a building full of microphones! The empty lot, midnight. If you really want to know."

It was Mulroy's turn to glare. "You setting me up for something? Why the empty lot?"

Tuck didn't answer, only shook his head pitifully.

With obvious growing vexation, Mulroy persisted, "Okay, why midnight?"

"Why not? Is it past your bedtime? Just come and meet me so we can get this over with. I'll tell you everything—as long as you keep my name out of it," he added, pivoting and pointing in Mulroy's face.

Mulroy stared into the man's eyes and saw the desperation he was trying to hide. "Of course," he said convincingly.

Thus assured, Tuck shoved Mulroy out of the room and shut the door, and he proceeded to drink in peace.

Mulroy trotted away, smirking. "Not just an intern for much longer," he whispered to himself.

* * *

Megan sobbed with relief as Cy and Nelly hurried to remove the gag and untie her. Once she was free, Megan threw her arms around Cy and buried her wet face in her front. "It's okay now," Cy soothed her, holding her tightly. "It's okay. We're gonna take you home."

Nelly cast a nervous glance at the light from the doorway. The sun was still up, but daylight was fading fast.

Finding her voice, Megan choked out, "He left me here. I couldn't get untied. I was stuck—he just left me!"

When the next wave of sobs had subsided, Cy took the girl by the shoulders and looked her in the eye. "Megan, *who* left you here?"

"I don't know. He had a ski mask on. He was hiding behind a tree on the short cut through the woods. He jumped out and put a stinky rag over my mouth, and it made me sleep. When I woke up, he was carrying me here. He left me, and he came back to check on me a little later—I heard him outside—but he didn't even come in."

"He didn't say anything to you?"

"No."

"Did you get a look at his eyes through the mask?"

"I tried, but whenever I looked, he kept squinting so I couldn't see them."

"Are you sure it was a man?" asked Nelly.

Megan nodded with certainty. "I could hear him breathing—he even growled sometimes," she said. Then she added, "Who are you?"

"This is Nelly. She's a friend," said Cy.

Nelly gave Megan a reassuring smile and asked, "Are you hurt? Can you walk?"

"I think so." Megan leaned on Cy as she stood, wincing at the soreness in her joints. She flexed her legs experimentally, shifting from foot to foot, before nodding.

"Good," said Nelly, "because the sun could set any time now, and after that we'll only have minutes of—"

Cy was puzzled by Nelly's abrupt silence—until she heard it, too: soft, crunching noises from just outside, getting nearer. Someone was approaching.

Megan started to gasp. Cy covered her mouth, then passed her off to Nelly, who held her close, huddled in a corner of the shack. The teenager flattened herself against the wall by the door, watching the suffused rectangle of light on the floor, where a faint shadow grew. The footsteps paused at the doorway.

Nelly could feel the child shaking in her arms. She gave her a gentle squeeze, wondering if she and Cy could hold off the kidnapper long enough for the girl to run away (to where?).

The figure remained paused in the doorway, apparently staring inside—perhaps regarding the spot where Megan had lain, wondering how she'd escaped and where she was hiding. Any moment now, the figure would turn and run off, pursuing the escaped victim, giving the women a chance to flee and hopefully bring the girl to safety...

The shadow stepped into the shack.

Cy bellowed and tackled the figure. In the dim light, together they looked like a giant, dark mass of flailing limbs. They crashed into one wall, then another. Something fell from the intruder's hand and clattered, then crunched as it was stepped on. "Run!" Cy shrieked, and Nelly started to pull a terrified Megan toward the door, but the figure spun and flipped Cy onto the ground, blocking the avenue of escape.

Nelly was terrified, but she wasn't about to let Cy be hurt without at least trying to fight back. Letting go of Megan, she started toward the assailant—

"Cy?!"

Cy, who had been struggling to free her arm from her opponent's tight grip, squinted in the dark. "Mom?!"

Nelly stopped short. Her eyes having adjusted, she could just make out the woman's ponytail, the badge on her chest. In a moment, the four of them were out of the shack, and it was difficult to tell whom Deputy Grogan was more surprised at having discovered: the missing child or her own daughter.

"How did you find us?!" Cy demanded to know once she'd explained how they'd ended up here.

"Deputy Grogan calling dispatch," Jen said into her radio. As she waited for a reply, she explained, "This is one of Pressler's properties. The sheriff sent us out to search them."

"Dad told me Mr. Pressler doesn't like me," said Megan. "Is Mr. Pressler the one who kidnapped me?"

"We don't know yet," said Jen. "This is Deputy Grogan calling dispatch. Can anyone hear me? I've found Megan, and we have an officer down on Route 127. Do you copy?" The only response was static.

"Maybe we're out of range," suggested Cy.

"The range on this is over thirty miles." Jen tried again. Still nothing. Giving up, she went back into the shack to retrieve the GPS device that had led her here…and emerged with a grim expression, holding a cracked, misshapen ruin of a gizmo.

Cy's face fell at the sight of it. "I'm sorry," she said, looking remorsefully at each of them in turn.

Jen sighed gravely. "I've walked too far through these woods to remember the way back to town. Unless one of you has a compass, we're going to have to camp in this shack tonight. I'm not risking any of us getting trapped out in the elements after dark, and there just isn't enough daylight left for us to find our way back. If we try, we're bound to get lost."

Megan started to cry anew. Jen put a hand on her shoulder. "I'm sorry, kiddo. I promise I'll get you to your parents tomorrow."

Cy regarded the suffering child who had been abducted and trapped, alone, for hours, convinced she'd been left to expire. In as confident a voice as she could muster, she said, "Mom, I think we *can* get home. Right now."

Jen looked at her evenly and said, "Do you have a compass? Because if not, then we've no choice—"

"We've got something better. We've got her."

Nelly blinked as she realized Cy was pointing in her direction. "What?" she stammered.

Cy turned to her. "Nelly, you knew exactly how to find this shack—but you couldn't have seen it from where we were."

"Yes, I could! I…" But even as she said it, as she summoned the image to the forefront of her memory, she searched it with her mind's eye…and the shack wasn't visible. *How…?*

"You knew it was there because you recognized the area— because you've been through it before. You came this way after you woke up next to the road. When you saw the area again, you remembered it—just like you remembered the SUV, after seeing it only once, passing us in the opposite direction! Nelly..." She stepped over and touched her shoulder. "You may have lost your memories, but I think your *memory*, itself, is, well, perfect."

Cy's blue eyes stared into Nelly's amber ones. Nelly remembered seeing those brilliant blue eyes for the first time, and it struck her how the memory felt just as clear and vivid as what she was seeing just this moment. Thinking back, nearly *every* memory she possessed felt that same way. No wonder she had such trouble distinguishing between past and present...

Jen clearly wasn't buying it. "Cy, believe me, I'm as desperate to get home as you are, but—"

"Mom, she can do it! You can!" Cy insisted, turning back to Nelly, who was shaking her head slowly.

"Cy, I don't remember coming this way. Even if you're right, even if I *can* remember everything I see and do, that doesn't mean I can just access those memories at will. Or if I can, I don't know how."

"That's just fear talking. You're scared of...of what you said before. And you're scared of failing. I get it. But I know you can do this!"

Jen was losing patience. "Cy—"

"Just answer me one question," Cy pressed, ignoring her mother. "Remember listening to the song 'Maneater' in the hospital?"

"Yes," said Nelly, bemused. "That's why you gave me the name—"

"And after you heard it, you realized you remembered the lyrics?"

"Right."

Cy gripped both of Nelly's shoulders. "When the song *first played*, could you remember the lyrics then?"

"Ye—" Nelly stopped. She remembered hearing the music, listening to the words of the song. Afterward, when she found she could recall every line, every verse, it felt to her as if the song were familiar. She *assumed* she'd heard it before. But no, as it played that first time, she hadn't known what words were going to come next. It was *new* then, and only felt familiar *after* the one experience—just as with everything else that had happened since she woke up...

"Cy, that's enough," said Jen. "We're not risking it, and that's final. If we hurry, we can gather some rocks, and I can at least make us a campfire—"

"Mom, please, just trust me! I've been with her all afternoon! She remembers stuff! I told you, she's memorized the quadratic equation!"

"I don't care. I'll keep trying my radio throughout the night, on the off-chance it starts working again. We'll set out at the first light of dawn. If we're lucky, it'll be a clear sky, and we'll use the sun to—"

"It's that way."

Jen and Cy turned to see Nelly pointing at what seemed a random direction through the woods.

Nelly turned back to Cy, and when she spoke, there was astonishment in her voice. "You're right. That was the first and only time I'd heard the song—I wasn't even paying close attention—and right away I had it perfectly memorized."

Cy grinned.

Jen was less enthusiastic. "You're saying Veil's in that direction?" she said icily.

"N-no," Nelly answered, quailing slightly under Jen's glare. "But that's the way I went when I passed through here, and I ended up in town eventually."

Jen stepped closer to her. "You would've been disoriented, confused, barely conscious."

"I was," agreed Nelly. "I was also in a lot of pain."

"Then how can you *possibly* remember your route?"

Nelly looked into the woman's face and saw that there was no convincing her. Who could blame her, when Nelly barely believed it, herself?

Her jaw trembled. "I'll go by myself, then," she said.

"What?"

Megan gave a little gasp. Even Cy was taken aback.

"You don't have to risk it," said Nelly. "You're responsible for them, not for me. I'll go by myself, and when I get to town, I'll tell the sheriff, and he can send someone back for you guys."

Only Cy knew her well enough to tell that, beneath her tough, skeptical expression, her mother was impressed. It was plain that Nelly was completely in earnest, but also that the idea of being alone in the forest, day or night, terrified her. And yet, for their sake, she was willing to risk her worst fear coming true.

The deputy looked again at the darkening sky and heaved a sigh of resignation. She gestured for Nelly to lead the way. As they fell into step behind the amnesiac, she muttered to Cy, "If this doesn't work, you're grounded."

IX

Perhaps it was because they feared nightfall would at any moment spring upon them before they made it out of the forest, but daylight lasted considerably longer than any of them expected. Nelly led them at a steady pace, focused on her surroundings, searching out anything that struck her as familiar. At one point she paused and shut her eyes, and chose her direction by feeling her way between the bushes, explaining that a stinging pain had forced her to close her eyes when she passed through this area. At another point she got down on her knees and crawled, citing a similar reason.

Jen maintained an awareness of their immediate area, lest the kidnapper or some dangerous animal be lurking nearby. Cy led Megan by the hand and kept up a stream of steady conversation with the girl, keeping her distracted and cheerful, which made Jen proud.

All at once, Nelly came to a halt. Jen looked up sharply. The conversation between Cy and Megan abruptly ceased. Jen stepped around them and circled Nelly, finding her staring at the ground, her facial muscles strained, her eyes bugged. "Nelly...?"

The young woman looked up at her with horror in her eyes. "I...c-can't remember any more."

Over Nelly's shoulder, Jen saw Megan go pale.

"I know I came this far. But...after that..."

Quickly Jen peered through the trees, straining for some sign of civilization. The sun had certainly set by now; they had only scant minutes of twilight left in which to see. The trees and bushes grew so thickly here that Jen couldn't make out more than a few meters in any direction.

"I'm sorry," Nelly said to Cy, who looked crestfallen. Megan tried to hold back more tears, but they rolled down her cheeks anyway. Cy held her close.

"Deputy Grogan calling dispatch. Over." Jen tried her radio twice more before giving up. "Cy, check your phone," she ordered.

Cy obeyed. "I've got one bar."

"Try calling the station."

Cy tried, but after a moment she shook her head. "The signal's not strong enough."

Jen sighed and scanned the area again. Barring the one they'd come from, no direction seemed better or worse than any other. Veil lay somewhere before them, hidden by wood growth and encroaching darkness. If they picked an angle at random, they might get lucky, or they might unknowingly dive straight back into the heart of the forest—

Something caught her attention. "Cy, bring your phone over here." Cy did so, activating the flashlight mode. By the light of the phone, Jen stared down at a familiar-looking log. Taking an angle from it, she turned her head in a particular direction. "Follow me," she said, and the four of them circumnavigated the log.

Seconds later, Jen pushed apart the branches of two trees and stepped out onto mown grass. A few feet ahead was paved ground. It was exactly the spot on Mountain Boulevard where Emma had brought her and the sheriff to see the "dead body." Nelly had led them as far as she had gone while conscious. Here she must have passed out, terminating her continuous memory.

Jen held the branches aside for the others, eliciting a shout of joy from Megan. Cy breathed a sigh of relief as she stepped out from the trees. She half-turned in Jen's direction, hesitated, then turned the other way to face Nelly. "You see?" she said. "I knew you'd get us out of there."

* * *

Deputy Benno was fine, they learned when they reached the station. He had radioed for help once he'd regained consciousness, and was taken to the hospital. Deputies were dispatched to the scene, but they found no trace of the silver SUV or its occupants.

Jen was with the sheriff now, repeating Cy and Nelly's account of the attack that took place on the old highway. The sheriff stood behind his desk, his brow furrowed, as he listened. He looked harried and fatigued. His eyes darted a glance through the glass in the door, and caught Nelly watching him. She looked away.

From here in the waiting area, where she sat with Cy, Nelly could see into several of the adjoining rooms. Next to the sheriff's office was a break room, where several tired, footsore deputies congregated and feasted on store-bought desserts, celebrating the successful end to their day-long search.

One deputy seemed to be in lower spirits than the others. He was tall, thin, thirtyish, with a pouty-looking mouth and mussy, light brown hair that looked as if it'd had the color drained out of it in patches. Earlier, when Jen had arrived at the station leading Megan by the hand, the deputies who had been here applauded for her—except this one, who merely glowered. Nelly wondered what his problem was.

Megan was at the back of the building with her father, who, although allowed to visit with her, was still under arrest, and therefore not allowed to leave the jail cells for the time being. A doctor had stopped by and examined Megan, and pronounced her dehydrated but otherwise physically fine, despite some skin abrasions on her wrists and ankles. Though she claimed not to be hungry, her father had gently persuaded her to eat some crackers and fruit.

Dispatch had been trying to get hold of Sandra Toombs, but apparently her search party had gotten lost and couldn't be reached. However, word of Megan's rescue had spread throughout the town within minutes, so as soon as her mother returned to civilization, she'd learn of it.

The station's front door burst open, and for a moment Nelly thought it would be the mother, but she recognized the two people who entered. They were...*Kurt Riner, attorney, running for mayor against Elijah Pressler,* she recalled, *and Amy Chester, Kurt's fiancée and campaign manager.* She'd glimpsed them hours earlier, for barely a few seconds, yet she could recall the details perfectly. As bleak as her situation was, she couldn't help but feel thrilled at this newfound ability.

The couple went straight to the sheriff's office door. Kurt started to knock, but Amy simply opened the door and marched in. Kurt followed her, looking somewhat abashed. "Keith," he nodded to the sheriff.

"Kurt." The sheriff returned the nod, all but pretending Amy wasn't there. "What brings you here?"

Before either of them could answer, the front door flew open again to admit a thin, forty-something woman in an expensive-looking winter coat, with long, jet-black hair and much makeup, some of which was smeared from crying. *This,* Nelly felt sure, had to be the mother—she even recognized facial features similar to Megan's. Indeed, when the woman hurried to Dubowski's office, the sheriff simply said, "Grogan," and Jen escorted the anxious woman to the door at the back.

"Megan!" The woman's voice caught as she charged inside. The door closed after her.

In reply to the sheriff's question, Kurt Riner said, "I'm anticipating you. I've learned that Megan was found at a property belonging to Elijah Pressler, and that three unidentified persons in a silver SUV were patrolling the area, more or less. Now, on the one hand, if Pressler's the kidnapper, maybe he's stupid enough to hide the kid in his own place where someone was bound to look for her, but on the other hand—"

"Mr. Pressler, in fact, authorized the search of his own properties," interrupted the sheriff, "albeit after the search had already begun."

"And you think that clears him," Amy said in a scathing voice.

The sheriff shrugged. "It's possible he'd learned we'd started searching his properties and said what he said to look innocent. Or it was his plan all along, and he wanted to take indirect credit for Megan's rescue."

"But then why the SUV?" asked Kurt.

The ghost of a smile played at his friend's lips. "I have an idea about that," the sheriff said.

After a long enough pause that it was obvious the sheriff wasn't going to elaborate, Kurt went on, "In any case, if I were in your shoes, I'd suspect someone might be out to frame Pressler."

"Pressler suspects exactly that, though he's inclined to point the finger at Greg Toombs, who I admit has a greater motive."

99

"Greater than the gain of winning the election?"

Amy cast an anxious glance at her fiancé. "Kurt, don't volunteer things like that!"

However, as before, Kurt and the sheriff were in silent communication that excluded her. In this case, each exchanged a subtle smile of amusement. "All right," said the sheriff after a moment. "You want me to interview you? Let's make it official." He circled the desk and closed the door, muting the conversation to those outside.

The deputies had all trickled out of the break room, leaving some of the goodies behind on a table. Cy gestured with her head and said, "I don't know about you, but I'm starving." Nelly was almost surprised to find that she, too, was hungry. The two of them crossed to the break room and besieged the leftovers.

For several minutes they ate in pensive silence. With their bellies full, it was easier to ponder and apply logic to what they knew. When Cy broke the silence, she unknowingly voiced the conclusion Nelly had also come to: "So even though you'd seen the shack, your memory loss couldn't have had anything to do with Megan's kidnapping. Not if whatever caused your memory loss happened all the way out on the old highway, where you woke up."

Nelly nodded. "It might not even have happened *there*. I might have been crawling for miles and miles before that."

On their way through the woods, Jen had promised that the sheriff's department would thoroughly investigate the area on County Road 127, but Nelly could already see it clearly in her memory. There was nothing to find there, no clue to her origin. As far as her mystery went, they'd hit a dead end.

Once again showing their thoughts were in sync, Cy said, "I'm sorry we haven't figured out who you are."

Nelly half-smiled. "We saved a missing girl. I'd say that's a fair trade-off." She reached out and took Cy's hand. "Thank you," she said. "You've—been great. I'm lucky you found me."

Cy smiled, touched. Simultaneously they moved in and hugged, and held each other for a long moment.

"What are you gonna do next?" Cy asked when they pulled apart.

"Well, your mom said she's going to find somewhere for me to stay tonight. Tomorrow we'll do the fingerprinting, and then…I guess social services will take over from there."

"I wouldn't—" Cy hesitated, then went on, "I wouldn't mind helping you some more."

"I know." Nelly smiled in appreciation. "But maybe instead you should focus on patching things up between you and your mom."

Cy's mood instantly soured. "It's hard to patch things up when she might be lying to me."

"You mean what Rob told you?"

"Yeah."

Nelly hesitated, wondering how deeply she should get involved, then she said, "It sounded to me like he was trying to drive a wedge between you and her—so he could manipulate you more easily."

"You think he was lying?"

It was at this exact point that Jen, returning from the jail cells, passed near enough to the break room door to overhear what was said within. Nelly replied, "I'm not sure. But I wouldn't work yourself up by looking into your dad's death—not unless *you* think there was something suspicious about it."

Jen halted as if she'd hit a brick wall, and she stood rooted there, eyes wide.

"No, I don't," Cy admitted, "but if I'm not helping you get your memory back, how can I think about anything *but* Dad's death?"

At that moment, the station's front door opened a third time. Jen jumped when Cy poked her head out of the break room door to see who it was, but Cy didn't see her mother.

Elijah Pressler strode in with his assistant just behind him.

Hoping Cy would assume she'd only just approached this second, Jen marched by her to greet him. "Can I help you, Mr. Pressler?"

"I'd like to see the sheriff," said Pressler in a slightly louder voice than was necessary.

"He's in an interview right now, but if you'll wait—"

The sheriff's office door opened and Amy emerged. Pressler gave a quick nod to his assistant, who stood to one side and began video-recording with his phone.

"Elijah," Amy drawled in a taunting voice. "Are you here to congratulate the sheriff for finding Megan?"

"Congratulate him, yes," said Pressler, putting on an air of restrained emotion and humility, "but, more importantly, to thank him—and you two as well. Because we were able to put aside our differences and work together, we managed to—"

By now, Amy had spotted the man recording this, and burst out, "Oh, give me a break, Pressler!"

Kurt touched her arm. "Amy, he's trying to bait us—"

"It wasn't us teaming up that got the kid back, it was the sheriff doing what he would've done anyway, with or without your help!"

"Well, exactly!" A subtle twinkling of the eye was the only hint that Pressler was enjoying this. "That's why I want to thank him! Please, I'm not looking for a fight!"

This only enraged Amy further. As Kurt continued to try to intervene, the argument erupted into a full-blown shouting match. Jen cast a questioning glance at the sheriff, who shook his head resignedly.

The noise attracted the attention of Sandra Toombs, who appeared from down the hall, then doubled back momentarily to tell her daughter to stay put. In the half-second that she looked away, Pressler made a quick gesture to his assistant to stop recording.

"You see?!" Amy screeched. "He doesn't care about cooperation or the kid being saved, he just wants to play the good guy to the voters and vilify his opponents!"

"Which you're helping him with immensely," Kurt muttered through clenched teeth.

As Sandra drew near, Pressler reached out tenderly. "Honey, is Megan okay?"

To his complete surprise, the woman held up a hand to ward him off. "Don't," she said in an icy tone, "call me honey."

Kurt and the sheriff looked almost as taken aback as Pressler. Amy looked as if she'd received an unexpected treat. Sandra noticed her expression but continued to address Pressler. "My ex-husband insists you're the one who took Megan. That you're jealous for attention."

Pressler's eyes seemed to enlarge as he said beseechingly, "You know I would never hurt Megan."

"No, Eli. I don't know that. That's the point. The same way I don't know for sure my ex-husband didn't do it, to try to frame you." Pressler looked confused, but before he could reply, she rounded on Kurt and Amy. "Or that your political opponents didn't do it, to try to embarrass you somehow. Or that someone in the sheriff's department didn't arrange it—though if they did, it would explain how a deputy just *happened* to find Megan in the middle of nowhere." Her wrathful gaze slid over to Jen.

No one around her could help feeling an urge to back away. Her barely contained fury was no act.

Only two people weren't quaking in their boots: Nelly and Cy. Not long after Mrs. Toombs had joined the others, Nelly found herself staring in a particular direction, her brain whirling, the pieces of the puzzle finally falling into place. When she looked at Cy, she saw an expression that mirrored her own dawning realization.

"You can't prove any of that!" spat Amy, more out of fear than derision.

"Prove it?" Sandra said in a deadly whisper. "Who said anything about *proving* it? Do I look like I care which one of you is guilty? Or to be more precise, that *only* one of you is guilty? I know it was one of you, and that's all I need. I am the richest person in this town. I have the power to ruin all of your lives. And I will. No more freedom for my ex-husband. No more running for mayor. No more sheriff's department. *I will bring you all down.* What do I care if I hurt innocent people along the way, as long as I get the one who *hurt my little girl?!!!* Still feel like smirking?" She directed this last at Amy, who looked torn between horror and haughty disbelief.

Into this sea of tension spoke a small voice: "Mom?"

Jen glanced over. "Not now, Cy."

"Nelly remembers."

Instantly all eyes were upon her. Cy swallowed and went on, "She saw the kidnapper put Megan in the shack before she blacked out."

She turned to Nelly, who extended her arm, her finger pointing. "It was him."

Six heads turned.

"Ernie??" said Pressler, dumbfounded.

Pressler's assistant froze in place for a moment, then he darted toward the front door. Jen intercepted him less than halfway there. The sheriff joined in a moment later to help restrain him.

X

"**B**ut wait," said Megan, "I thought you said Nelly passed by the shack really early in the morning. That was before he...he put me there. How could she have seen him?"

"She didn't," said Cy. "It was a trick."

They were sitting together in the break room. Ernie, having confessed rather promptly, had been taken to the cells. The shouted threats and profanities of his fellow inmate had since died down. Kurt Riner and Amy Chester had departed. Megan's mother was with the sheriff in his office, and Jen was in another room interviewing Mr. Pressler.

"We tricked him the same way he tried to trick us, by telling us he'd seen Nelly at the furniture store—when really she was passed out by Mountain Boulevard," Cy explained.

"Why did he say he saw her at the store?"

"Well, he knew the spot where Emma first saw Nelly is in the direction of the shack, so he was worried maybe Nelly *had* seen him. So he led us somewhere else on the other side of town."

"So she wouldn't get her memory back?"

"Right. And it also gave him an alibi, saying he was there when he was really abducting you."

Nelly returned from the kitchen area just then, holding a cup of hot chocolate, which she gave to Megan. As the girl sipped, she murmured, "I'm glad you figured out who did it."

Nelly patted Megan on the back. "You helped us figure it out, you know."

"Me?"

"You told us the kidnapper kept growling and squinting through his ski mask. He was really doing that because he had trouble seeing—without his glasses that he normally wore. He couldn't wear his glasses and the mask at the same time."

"Ohhh."

* * *

"Then are we done?" asked Pressler in a friendly tone, flashing his bright teeth.

Are our choices for mayor really down to this guy and my high school tormentor's beau? thought Jen. "Yes, we are," she said, standing. "You're free to go."

"Good," said Pressler. "Now that we've established that I knew nothing about what Ernie did, I have a question for you: why did Ernie do it? Or hasn't he said?"

Jen leveled a stern glare at him. "Mr. Pressler, you're well aware I can't talk about such things."

Pressler leaned back. "No, of course not. Well, I'll just have to figure it out for myself, then."

"Feel free." Jen opened the door for him.

But Pressler hadn't moved from his chair. "We know the motive wasn't ransom. He hid the girl in a property belonging to me, but perhaps that was just because it was an expedient location—as my assistant, he knows about all my properties. I suppose he also figured I'd send the sheriff to search those properties, so she'd be found."

"Mr. Pressler—"

"Ernie's always seemed to like Sandra, so I doubt he did it to hurt her. But I can't see how he'd profit from—wait..." His mouth curled up into an admiring smile. "No. No way." He stood up. "He's in love with her, isn't he? With my girlfriend! He kidnapped Sandra's daughter to bring about exactly what happened—but it went further than he expected. He wanted her to suspect both me *and* her ex-husband. With the two of us out of the picture, he thought he might have a chance. Ha!" He swaggered over to Jen, shaking his head. "I never gave him enough credit."

Dubowski appeared in the doorway. "You done, Grogan?"

"Yes, sir." Scowling, Jen followed Pressler out.

Sandra approached her. "I wanted to thank you for rescuing my daughter," she said. "And I'm sorry if I made you feel threatened earlier. As a fellow mother, you understand."

"No worries, ma'am," Jen said tightly.

"I also wanted to thank *your* daughter, Cyanne."

"You should be thanking Nelly," Cy said, coming up to them. "We never would've gotten out of the forest if it weren't for her."

Nelly was still in the break room with Megan. One by one they came in and thanked her—first the sheriff, then Sandra, and finally Pressler. "Sounds like you're the hero of the hour," he said to her after Megan left the room with her mother.

Nelly shrugged. "Just in the right place at the right time."

Pressler nodded, but it seemed he was nodding to himself, looking her up and down appraisingly. Nelly found it disconcerting, especially now that they were alone.

"If you'd been anywhere else, things would've gone badly for me," he said. "You gave the story a happy ending. I'll have to think of something to give you in return."

Nelly did not know what he meant by that, and wasn't sure she wanted to.

Pressler tipped an imaginary hat and trotted away.

* * *

"Mom," said Cy once they were alone, "I need to ask you something."

"Me, too. What do you think about Nelly coming to stay with us? At least for a while."

Cy stared at her, a wide grin spreading across her face. "Are you serious?"

"Well, like you said, she did lead us to safety. I think it's the least we can do."

Cy was so touched, she couldn't speak. She darted forward and, for the first time in months, hugged her mother. It lasted two and a half seconds. Then Cy broke away and said, "I'll go tell her."

Once she was gone, Jen quickly wiped her eyes.

* * *

"Go wait in the car, sweetie," said Sandra. Megan waved goodbye to Pressler and left him and her mother on the front steps of the sheriff's station.

"Look," he said, "it's all right. You've been through a tough ordeal. I understand why you said what you did. I forgi—"

"We're not seeing each other anymore," she cut in.

He stared at her for a moment. "Excuse me?" His voice had just the slightest menacing edge.

"You might not have known it was Ernie, but you suspected someone was setting you up. You had a hunch where Megan was all along. You sent three goons in a silver SUV to check, and they did. Megan heard them. She thought it was her abductor coming back to check on her."

"If I'd found her, I would've brought her home!"

"No. You were worried that if you rescued her too soon, your voters might suspect you kidnapped her, yourself, and then rescued her to play the hero. You let her lie there, tied up, hungry, terrified.

"You planned to send the sheriff there, later, by telling him to search all your properties. In the meantime, you sent your goons to patrol Route 127 in their SUV. Since there was no ransom demand, you expected the kidnapper to try to play the hero, himself, and Route 127 is the closest road to the shack. But your goons misunderstood your instructions. You just wanted them to *observe* who set you up. They thought you wanted them to catch him. So when that poor deputy pulled off the road..."

Pressler took the woman by the shoulders. She went rigid but didn't resist. He said, "I promise you that's not what happened."

She gave a small smile. "Maybe not that exactly, but I know it's close enough. You're very good at telling misleading truths."

Anger darkened Pressler's features. "You didn't come up with this all on your own. Who put these ideas in your head?"

The woman's eyes flicked to the side for an instant before she backed out of Pressler's grip. "Megan's father was right," she said. "You've always been jealous of the attention I give her. Well, now you have good reason to be."

In a few moments she was gone, leaving a furious Pressler staring after her. Slowly he turned to face the direction in which she had glanced. He found himself staring at Dubowski, watching from his office window. The sheriff gave him a long look, half pity, half warning, before he moved out of sight.

His remark about the sheriff having been a forest ranger— *that,* Pressler realized, was where he had given himself away.

Despite his diatribe against Greg Toombs, Pressler had believed at the time that it was *Dubowski* who had kidnapped Megan in order to set him up. His associates had verified Megan was being held in an old ranger's station, which seemed to confirm the theory. But when he'd hinted to the sheriff that he knew the girl's location, Dubowski's eyes had told him he had no idea what Pressler was getting at. In the end, it had backfired.

Pressler remained where he was a minute more, his gaze locked on the sheriff's window. An eerie calm settled over him before he turned and marched off into the night.

* * *

Nelly, riding with Jen and Cy, was confused when they drove out of Veil, but then remembered, in the hospital, how Cy had mentioned her home was too far away to walk. Almost six miles out of town, they arrived at the Grogans' house. It was difficult to see, now that night had fallen, but Nelly could at least make out that it was three stories tall—much bigger than she'd expected.

Her surprise must have shown, for Jen said, "Technically it isn't ours. The man who owns it is sort of my godfather. He said Cy and I could house-sit while he's visiting New Zealand."

"When does he come back?"

"He wasn't sure. He told me to ask again in fifteen years."

They pulled into a two-car garage attached to the side of the house. Curiosity tugged at Nelly's senses, fueling the urge to explore this vast abode, but after the long day's events those senses were sluggish and dim. Blearily she followed Cy and Jen into the house and up the stairs, where she waited while they scavenged for clean sheets and towels with which to prepare a spare bedroom.

As Nelly stood there, gazing vacantly at the next flight of

stairs leading to the third floor, she felt something soft rubbing her hand. Where a moment before there had been empty space, a calico cat had materialized. It sat on the banister, nuzzling her with its head. "Aw," Nelly cooed.

Cy came out of the bedroom and smiled. "That's Roswell," she said. "He's a love bug."

Nelly blinked. "Did you say, he? But it's a—" But Cy had already gone down the hall, out of earshot. Nelly turned back to the cat and scratched under his chin. "Roswell," she murmured. "Funny name. I wonder why they call you that."

The cat opened its jaws. "Mmeep." Nelly's eyebrows went up. The noise he'd made was at quite a low pitch for a cat, and wasn't quite a meow.

Again the creature uttered, "Mmmeeep."

"Nelly?" Jen appeared and gestured into the room. "It's ready. Come on in."

The bed was full-size, facing sideways against the wall beneath a large window divided into several square panes. Beyond that, Nelly was too tired to take in any more details.

Jen was clearly fatigued as well, yawning as she set some pajamas on the bed. "I think these'll fit you," she said. "Cy can show you where the bathroom is."

"Jen," said Nelly as she started to leave. "Thank you. I appreciate this so much. This is so generous."

Jen smiled back, but it seemed somewhat forced. "Don't mention it," she said.

Nelly assumed she was just eager to get to bed.

* * *

Cy turned on the faucet in the bathroom and closed the door. "Rob," she said into her cell phone, "you have to stop calling me. And no, this isn't *my* last chance, it's yours. Because I *will*

112

tell Mom about you, and you know she'll run you out of town. Hell, you're lucky if that's *all* she does," she added, thinking of Mrs. Toombs.

"*I'm just gonna tell you one thing about your dad,*" said her ex's slick voice, "*then we'll see if you don't want to know more—*"

"No, Rob! This is why I broke up with you! I mean, don't you think I'm having a hard enough time already?! Or do you just not care? I tell you you're hurting me, and you twist things to try to make me think there's something wrong with me for—"

"*I told you, I'm not gonna just let you win because you're a girl.*"

"I don't need your validation to know I'm right. I might not know a lot about relationships, but I do know they shouldn't feel like this, like there's a winner and a loser. I'm done with you."

"*Then I guess you don't really care about your dad after all.*"

Cy nearly flung the phone into the bathtub. "You're gonna die alone, Rob," she snapped before she hung up.

A few minutes later, she returned to Nelly's room with a toothbrush still in its store packaging. "Hope you remember how to use one of these," she said lightly.

Perhaps too lightly. "Are you okay?" Nelly asked from where she was sitting on the bed.

Cy nodded quickly. "Yeah, I'm fine. Um, we can find you some more clothes tomorrow. I bet Azura's things will fit you."

"Azura?"

"My sister. She's a scientist, doing a sort of internship in Antarctica. We still have a lot of her stuff." Thinking to herself a moment, she added, "I gotta call her back and apologize for blowing her off today."

"Antarctica. Wow." Nelly sounded distant, tense.

Cy went and sat by her. "What's wrong?"

Nelly shook her head dismissively. "Just a little wound up. Lots of different feelings. Thankful—for you and your mom. Nervous about tomorrow. Scared we won't find out who I am, even with the fingerprinting. Worried that I've lost...well, that's just it, I have no idea what I've lost. It could be good, it could be bad, and I don't even know which would be worse."

Cy said uncertainly, "Are you asking for help or do you just need me to listen?"

After a moment, Nelly gave a small chuckle. "Actually, I think you listening already helped. Just saying it out loud, I feel less twisted up."

"Good." Cy put an arm around her. "I'm glad you said that, because I got nothin'."

They both laughed. Nelly leaned her head on Cy's shoulder.

A minute later, Nelly felt ready to go to sleep. As Cy headed toward the door, she yawned and said, "Goodnight, Nelly."

"Ummm..."

Cy turned back.

Nelly was making a face. "I've actually changed my mind. I'm not feeling great about that name."

"Oh! Okay, no problem. We'll just, um..." Cy stared at her friend for a moment, thinking. "How about...Violet?"

The young woman's face lit up. "Violet...yeah! I like that! That feels just right."

Cy nodded sleepily. "Good."

"How did you come up with that?"

"Hm? Oh, your hair."

Violet blinked. "My hair?" Puzzled, she lifted a lock in front of her face and squinted. "It looks dark brown to me."

Cy's mouth slowly dropped open. "Have you looked in a mirror since...?"

114

Violet gave a little shake of her head.

Cy offered her her hand. Violet took it and found she was trembling.

Cy led a hesitant Violet into the bathroom. She positioned her before the mirror, then turned on the light.

Violet found herself staring at a complete stranger with amber eyes and dark hair—dark, she noticed, except for a bright purple streak on one side. The stranger stared back in wonder and fascination, touching her mouth, her ears, her nose, turning her head from side to side slowly.

The stranger leaned toward Violet and asked her, "Who are you?"

Epilogue

Tuck Fleagle was late.

Rob Mulroy stamped his feet in the cold and scanned the breadth of the parking lot where, hours earlier, the farmers' market had been held. At least, while waiting, he'd finally figured out why Fleagle had named midnight as the meeting time: a few minutes before the hour, the gas station attendant across the street had clocked out for the night. The area was now completely deserted. On the other hand, Rob still had no idea what made this particular location Fleagle's top choice for a meeting place. What was he missing? Rob liked knowing more than others did. It almost always gave him an advantage. He'd thought it would give him with one with Cy. Her words continued to aggravate him. Maybe he couldn't get her back, but he could still prove she should've listened to him. Once he was a real reporter, he'd be able to reach hundreds of people at once, tell them all—

A figure shuffled into view from around the corner of the old grocery store. Rob shook his head in disbelief. "Seriously? You walked here?"

Fleagle stumbled up to him and gave a tipsy snicker. "I've lived in Veil all my life. I know all the backyard alleys and shortcuts—useful to a man who doesn't want to be followed."

Among the many things that convinced Rob he'd be the perfect reporter, one of them was his instinct for good stories. Where this lead was concerned, that certainty was fast beginning to fade. "You think people are following you?"

Fleagle chuckled humorlessly. "And there it is."

"There *what* is?"

"Little punk. You think you're the first to look at me and write me off? 'Crazy old man with his delusions and conspiracy theories.' Used to care what people like you thought of me—till I realized it's a waste of my time. I am what I am. Can't change me and I can't change you. So..." He leaned back against a nearby post and attempted to cross his arms, but his coordination was off. "Let's get this over with."

Rob could smell the alcohol on his breath. "This was a mistake," he said bitterly, turning to leave.

"Hey," drawled Fleagle, "I tried to tell you that when I first met you, remember? I knew you wouldn't believe me—no one ever does. But you're here now and I'm here, so we might as well talk, all right?"

Rob regarded him skeptically. Try as he might, he couldn't convince himself that this was anything but a fanciful, drunken old man. But the amnesiac girl—she was different. Rob was certain there was something extraordinary about her. If Fleagle knew anything about her at all, perhaps at least enough to point him in the right direction...

Rob turned back to him. "Okay," he said. "Tell me what you know."

Fleagle drew a deep breath, opened his mouth...and let his breath out slowly, staring off in a random direction.

Rob waved a hand in front of his eyes. "Hey, Fleagle? What are you doing?"

"I'm trying to decide just how to word this so I sound over-dramatic and kooky."

Rob marched off.

"Hey, do you wanna know who the girl is or not?"

Rob hated being toyed with. He wheeled around and hissed through clenched teeth, "Who is she then?"

Fleagle's expression turned grave. "The girl with no memory of her past possesses a secret that will shake the town of Veil to its core. It's her destiny to bring down a great evil that's festered here for years. Their showdown is inevitable—" He broke off suddenly, twisting his head all around.

"What? What is it?"

"Someone's here! Someone followed us!" He shot an accusatory look at Rob. "Followed *you!*"

"No one followed me!" Rob snapped, losing his temper.

"Yes, they did! They want to stop me from telling you!"

"Telling me what? Who's 'they?!' Hey!" As Fleagle started to run, Rob seized him by the back of his coat and twisted him around.

"Let me go! They'll kill me!"

"Just tell me—"

"Let me go—"

A sound like a thunderclap split the air, echoing out over the parking lot.

Both men froze, staring at each other in shock. As one, they turned their gazes down to regard the blood dribbling onto the ground between them. They looked up at each other one last time before one of them loosened his grip and slid to the pavement, never to move again.

Tuck Fleagle stared with mounting horror at Rob Mulroy's corpse. He didn't move, knowing there was no point in running. He waited, trying to will the fear away so that he might take some comfort in his last moments...

But more and more moments passed and there was no second thunderclap. Fear gave way to confusion. Fleagle turned on the spot. No sign of the shooter, of course. No sign of any third party, save for the grisly evidence beside him.

Finding his voice, he croaked, "I—I don't understand! Why him? Why him and not me?!?"

At first there was no answer. Then, as a chill breeze picked up, like a hideous song carried on the wind, a faint peal of laughter tickled Fleagle's ears. His hair stood on end at the sound: a cold, cruel cackling, a melody of sadistic mirth. The wind masked the direction from which the laughter came, so that it seemed to come from everywhere at once.

All rational thought died within Tuck Fleagle. Heedless of his direction, he fled.

The laughter echoed on…

WINTER IN VEIL

A Mystery Novella Series
by Miles Ledoux

Next time in Veil…

Candy was headed straight for the purple car Violet had noticed earlier. She was unlocking it, reaching for the door handle.

"Wait—wait!!"

Cy watched, bewildered, as Violet bolted down the steps.

"Wait, don't—"

Candy opened the door a moment before Violet plowed into her, knocking her over. In the next instant, with a loud *pop*, a gallon of blood geysered out of the car through the open door, cascading over the spot where Candy had been standing.

About the Author

Miles Ledoux was born in upstate New York and started writing murder mysteries at the age of nine. His first paid writing gig was in 2007, when a local theatre chose one of his plays for their summer melodrama. He received other royalties after moving to Los Angeles for graduate school, where he wrote, directed, and produced several mystery dessert theatre plays. He also started a side business designing and running mystery party games while working as a martial arts instructor.

Currently the author resides in Springfield, Vermont. Despite having lived in five different states, he has remained active in community theatre as a playwright, director, and actor. He also has a YouTube channel where he compares Agatha Christie adaptations to the books they were based on. His handle is @MysteryMiles.

Miles loves books, cats, music, Star Trek, Peanuts, and owns an ever-growing number of variations of the board game Clue. His favorite author is Lloyd Alexander.

You can connect with me on:

🌐 https://www.ledouxmysteries.com

www.ingramcontent.com/pod-product-compliance
Lightning Source LLC
Chambersburg PA
CBHW070753120626
46557CB00002B/577